Tit for Tat

by the same author

NO MAMA NO
CHILDREN CROSSING

Tit for Tat

Verity Bargate

JONATHAN CAPE
THIRTY BEDFORD SQUARE
LONDON

First published 1981
Copyright © 1981 by Verity Bargate
Jonathan Cape Ltd, 30 Bedford Square, London WC1

British Library Cataloguing in Publication Data

Bargate, Verity
Tit for tat.
I. Title
823'.914[F]

ISBN 0-224-01908-2

Photoset by Rowland Phototypesetting Limited
Bury St Edmunds, Suffolk
Printed in Great Britain by St Edmundsbury Press
Bury St Edmunds, Suffolk

For Eileen

One

I met my mother properly when I was eleven. She had just returned from a holiday that had begun as she waved goodbye to me eight years before. And now, husband number three beside her, she was ready to impress. In public, preferably, since she could now afford the clothes. Thus, nearly four weeks after the boat docked from Australia, they came to collect me from my convent boarding school. I had displeased her by running up to another mother by mistake, so the koala bear was withheld from me at first. It was prizegiving so we spoke only briefly. 'My darling child, how you've grown,' she said, smiling towards Princess Marie-Louise's back. 'Such a big girl. This is your new Daddy. We're going to have such fun.' No other introduction and as I put out my hand to shake his, they turned and walked away and I was hurried off to my seat. Returning to that same seat clutching my first prize, I looked over towards my mother to see what pride looked like. She didn't seem to know either, for she was kissing the man who had no name.

Saying goodbye to the nuns for ever was difficult when the convent had been my only home for eight years, both during term time and in the holidays. Sister Theresa cried; I didn't.

So Mummy and Daddy and Baby makes three went

home to the big new house. It was so full of silence they didn't need much furniture.

In due course I started my new school and the misery at home mattered less. I had never been to a day school before and, unprepared for the warmth and welcome extended to me, came close to relaxing into contentment. If only four p.m. had not been quite so unavoidable.

The husband was called Jock, which is perhaps why my mother called him nothing. There were strange unknowable things between those two that made me want to push my two bumps back inside my ribcage and lock it.

I had to do my homework at the walnut dining table, a piece of thick felt provided to protect the veneer from scholastic contamination. Quite often they would come in for more drinks or to play the piano and sing 'La Vie en Rose'. They were always kissing in those early days, right beside me, although they did have a five-bedroomed house at their disposal. Often I was forced to concentrate on concentrating and not the work. I never forgot that noise but it was only after Tim that I realised what had sounded so terribly wrong. It was too wet to convey genuine erotic intent; they seemed to be paddling in each others' mouths. Besides, they had separate bedrooms, Eva's large and comfortable, Jock's small and rather stale.

I had to make his bed some days. Everything I loathed was concentrated in that room and in bending over hospital corners to inhale his essence. Even stealing from the small change lying around brought no sense of triumph or achievement. It was too easy.

One day, while I was changing for hockey, a girl called Janet Brown came over.

'Hi, Sadie. We think you ought to wear a bra. We all do, and you're one of us. O.K.? Thought that was an

8

amazing save last week, when you stuck your stick out, low, not looking. If I went deaf that's what I'd miss, that sound of the ball, crack. So good, that noise.'

'Thanks, Jan. After this match I'm bringing out a record. The A side is Crack. Crack. Crack. Great balls I have stopped. The B side is silent. Great balls I have not stopped.'

She laughed and I turned and put my leg up to fasten my pads. At the convent these had been considered a luxury and it had been the custom for the girl who displeased the nuns the most during the week to play in goal. Saturday after Saturday I was the chosen one, even when it was so foggy I couldn't see the end of my stick, let alone the ball. I did, however, become an astonishingly good goalkeeper after a couple of winters of purple shins.

It was nearly a week before Eva and I were in the same room without Jock's bulk making everything unsayable. My throat was dry. I felt lumpy and plain beside the oft-bartered bride.

'Mother,' I said, and then corrected myself. She didn't like being called mother, said it made her feel old, but I still found it hard to say her name. It seemed disrespectful. I cleared my throat for my mistakes were now twofold as I never, ever spoke first.

'Eva, I mean.' She turned her face towards me but although the eyebrows were arched for questioning, her eyes were somewhere else.

'The girls at school say that I should . . .'

'?'

' . . . wear . . .'

'??'

' . . . a . . .'

'???'

' . . . bra.'

9

At least now she was looking at me. 'A what?'

'A bra. Brassière.'

'Ah. Do you know about periods?'

'Ummm . . .'

'You do, don't you?' she said accusingly.

'Well, a bit . . . But not why or where, really. Or quite which hole.'

'You don't need to know. And your language is common. Coarse . . . I'll get everything you need. The important thing when you change the pad is to wrap the old one in newspaper and burn it in the boiler.'

She closed the door behind her and I was left wondering why she hadn't wrapped me up in newspaper and burned me in the boiler.

When I came home from school the next day my bed looked like a sterile dressing trolley with various packets and rubber gloves. No sutures, surprisingly. Ice cream cone cornet bras were the fashion at school. Not salmon pink Aertex. After so often turning away to hide my nipples, I was now going to have to turn my back to hide the object which was supposed to make my embarrassment redundant. I tried one on and looked in the mirror. The shapeless pink patches looked like a skin graft.

The sanitary towels next. I opened the packet, took one out. There must be some mistake: this couldn't be right, this nosebag. I would be unable to walk.

During the summer holidays my breasts started to hurt and I was afraid. My body seemed to be becoming someone else's and I felt uncomfortable, as though I was a squatter. Pubic hair was tricky, too. I had thought it possible the hair heralded the arrival of a penis. And why was it curly when my own hair was straight? And should I use shampoo?

At the convent we had had to put our nightdresses on over our clothes before we undressed. It made us very dexterous, but it did take a long time. Now I reverted to the habit and that made it possible to be me again and not this undesirable alien.

I longed for the holidays to be over so that I could belong to a school once more and be recognised as a living person. It would be good to talk again, too, without fear of saying the wrong thing making me inarticulate. Perhaps I would be able to talk to someone like my English teacher who used to call me her walking dictionary and lent me her own copy of *The Old Man and the Sea*, someone who would explain all these things to me. Only another week.

I wished that the pile of newspapers my mother had provided me with had not been the *Financial Times*. It seemed mercenary.

And then the blood came and I wished I was grown up. It wasn't red enough at first to be convincing; it didn't seem alive the way blood usually was when it came from a cut. This, in my knickers and on the loo paper, looked inert, starved of oxygen. Fear made me aware of a source of sensation I had not known existed and would not recognise again until Tim and desire located it so violently that I wondered why God had made anywhere else register pain.

Back in my bedroom I went through my books looking for anything that might contain more information, but even as I was looking I knew I would have remembered. Old favourites like *The Four Feathers*, *Pride and Prejudice* and *Titus Groan* were not concerned with bleeding schoolgirls, and even *East Lynne* was wise after the event. *Pears' Encyclopaedia* was the only chance left after the dictionary said that a period was a full stop. But there was nothing under P and I couldn't think what else it might be under. I felt incredibly guilty suddenly, as though I was sullying the book, tarnishing it.

I had never before considered that perhaps my whole future would be lonely like today.

My fear was replaced by anxiety about the fit of the sanitary towels. They weren't the kind of thing one normally tried on so I hacked off about a third, oversewed the end and replaced the loops. So much for needlework prizes. I made myself wait a whole hour before going back to the lavatory, but it was no good. I was confronted with the end of my childhood and redder blood.

Jock rattled the door and told me to hurry up, although there were two other bathrooms, so my hatred of him even intruded on the first privacy I had ever been aware of needing. I was clumsy and slow with the belt and the hooks and the loops and ended up feeling like a horse-less jockey in a nappy.

If Jesus really did die for me I wish He'd asked me first, I wrote in my diary later; and later still, This must be the real Sign of the Cross. That was the day Jock started working in the kitchen, books and papers all over the table, the day that I needed to go through to the boiler room. My screwed-up newspaper package went back upstairs with me. I had never voluntarily entered a room that contained him unless by accident. He was there before me again the next morning, and throughout the day and evening, so I had to put the packages in a cupboard above my wardrobe. I wondered why the *Financial Times* was pink.

After that I gave up creeping downstairs to see if the coast was clear and simply put them all up in the cupboard. I'd never seen Jock work before. All I had ever registered him doing had been sucking my mother's mouth and carving a joint until it bled and then tipping the blood into the gravy boat.

Back to school in two days. The thought lessened the embarrassment of my imagined smell, the apparent secondary navel the hook and loop gave me and even made the unfamiliar chafing soreness seem bearable, as though this first acknowledged sensation between my legs, of pain, might be only temporary. A new trunk had appeared on the landing and I had twice banged my shin on it. The pile of *Financial Times*'s had discernibly diminished. At last more blood was remaining in my veins than was leaving from elsewhere and even the sun was shining again.

Eva came into my room. 'Help me bring your trunk in,' she said. When it was filling the space between the bed and the door my mother opened it. My clothes, in neat piles.

'New school this afternoon. You'll really love it. Your uniform is hanging up. Pack anything else you want to take in this top bit. It's a long drive and he's busy, so be ready when he calls. Won't boarding school be fun again? No more waiting for the bus. Lunch soon, before you go.'

And so I moved on again. Another town, another school, another dormitory, another repository for unwanted minors.

I went back to the house of silence once, at half term. Eva and Jock, meeting me at the station, enveloped me with their indifference, which seemed to embrace each other as well now. As we got to the front door they moved in on either side of me in a way that was nasty rather than frightening. It was nearly stimulating. Up the stairs. My bedroom door sealed with newspaper round the jamb. *Financial Times* again. Jock opened the door. The room really smelled. A foul heavy decaying smell.

I half expected to see somebody dead on my bed. Eva pointed to the cupboard above the wardrobe and, remembering, I wished myself the corpse. Jock put his thick arm up and opened the door to reveal the crumpled pink packages.

I looked at the floor, a scarlet lady.

'I told you to burn them,' said Eva. 'Being a woman is dirty enough, God knows, without you making it contagious. We've hardly been able to breathe in the house for weeks.'

'Actually,' said Jock, 'you're a dirty little bitch. We've had no social life.'

I didn't cry: my magenta face just had tears superimposed on it.

'Your mother has fainted twice. I've had to go out to get away from the stink. And now we have had to change our newspaper. It has become impossible to make sense of the *Financial Times*: you've defiled it. How dare you change our way of life? Anyone would think we were here for your convenience. Dirty bitch. What were you saving them up for? Guy Fawkes?'

I couldn't believe this was happening. I reached up for the parcels, standing on a chair. 'I don't want them dropped on the stairs either. And you'll have to light the boiler. It went out.'

I saw a carrier bag near the window and stepped down to get it. It contained a Bible, a Palm Sunday cross and a tube of Valderma, and as I filled it up I kept retching. Jock threw some matches at me and left the room. Eva spoke. 'I had to do it this way. You had to see, smell, for yourself. You would never have learned if I had written to you. You learn from your own experience, not anyone else's. Remember that. Being a woman is messy and complicated and dirty. You'll learn that.'

I got down from the chair. Eva held out her arms to me and I backed away, feeling afraid at last. She spoke again.

'Never forget that I did this for you. I did it because I love you.'

Two

Jock and Eva went abroad again about a month after that and I did not see either of them again until I was eighteen and in my last term at school. I received occasional postcards from exotic places, but there was never an address for me to write to.

Then suddenly one day the headmistress called me into her study and told me that they were back in England, my mother was in hospital and I was required to go and look after the dogs as the daily help was on holiday. I was taking my A levels at the time but my pleas to be allowed to sit my exams fell on deaf ears since this school's function was more to make life easier for reluctant parents than to educate their offspring, who did not, after all, pay the fees.

Jock and Eva, returning from further travels abroad, had settled into a house that was much smaller, a house for two people only. I had to sleep on the settee with the dogs, which was rather nice since they were affectionate towards me, somewhat to Jock's disgust. I was alone with them most of the time and we went for long walks through the Cotswold countryside together until they were exhausted, and then after I had fed them they fell into a contented stupor and I read until I, too, fell asleep. Sometimes I would hear Jock staggering in late, drunk, but most of the time he didn't come home at all. He wouldn't let me see my mother and I was too afraid even to ask him what was wrong with her or indeed which hospital she was in.

After I had been there ten days he appeared one lunchtime and told me in a rather irritated voice that for some reason my mother wanted to see me. I could not recall her ever wanting to see me before and felt nervous and apprehensive on the silent drive to the hospital, wondering what I had done wrong.

As we entered her room I was shocked by two things. The first was how very ill she looked and the second was that she appeared really pleased to see me. It was the only time we seemed to recognise each other, looking at each other's eyes without flinching, almost as though we shared a memory. She knew she was dying: I did not. I wanted to touch her, say something, but Jock's presence, as always, silenced me, so I just stood there looking around the room thinking how red the blood dripping into her arm was and how white her face. And then Jock left the room abruptly and we were precipitated into an embarrassed confrontation that left us no time for preparation.

Eva gestured to the drawer of her locker that, stupidly, was on the same side as her drip. I opened it for her and saw only her familiar crocodile handbag. I passed it swiftly to her as she seemed on the verge of panicking. Before she opened it she gestured to me that I should stand between her and the round window in the door. Fumbling, she withdrew an envelope with my name on it and pushed it towards my pocket with a silent 'Ssshh'. Then she spoke for the first time and her voice was low and fast and urgent – nothing cool or sophisticated about her now.

'If he comes in, change the subject. But in that envelope are some keys. Address is on them. He never knew about it. My flat. For you. Also the name of a solicitor. Not his, mine. He has all the papers. Ring him soon. I've signed everything but you must sign too, before anything happens to me or Jock finds out. All paid for. Just rates and bills for you. And when you move in, ring someone called Chris. Details in there. But only when you move in. Talk to the solicitor tomorrow. Promise me. Ssshh. He's coming.'

And I could only stay silent, my fingers feeling the shape of the keys through the envelope in my pocket, watching my mother's eyes and feeling a desolate sense of loss as Jock loomed up behind me.

'Time to go. You've tired your mother out. She's supposed to be resting. Look at her now.'

I was looking, and thinking how much prettier and bright-eyed she looked. I had never noticed that her eyes were green.

'I'll put your bag back for you,' I said, smiling.

'Why did you get it out?' Jock demanded in an angry voice.

Eva said wearily, 'We were looking for tissues, that's all.'

'But they're always here on the side.'

'I know. But they had fallen on the floor. We couldn't see them. Sadie was trying to be helpful.'

'Sadie was?'

Eva closed her eyes briefly. She looked very tired now.

'Say goodbye now, Sadie. It's school again for you tomorrow. Mrs Fisher will be back to help. Those dogs really love her.'

I held my mother's hand, felt again the pressure of recognition. I wanted to bend over and whisper in her ear. Anything. Even 'I love you', if that would have had a chance of sounding real and continuing this process I felt we had just begun. But Jock's heavy presence made the room seem short of oxygen: it was hardly possible to breathe now, let alone speak. I pressed my lips against her cheek as I had so often been required to do in the past, nothing given or exchanged, so that when now for the first time in my life I wanted the gesture to be real, it was too late, I didn't know how to make it. The only instinct that came to my aid made me clumsily press Eva's fingers so hard that she almost cried out in pain.

'Do be careful,' said Jock, 'you've overtired her. And hurry up. I'll drive you back.'

I stood up and looked at Eva once again; perhaps it wasn't too late. ''Bye Mother. We break up in four weeks so I'll see you then, if not before. And of course, now that I know where you are, I'll write.'

She kissed my hand and said, in a gentle voice she had never used to me before, 'Remember what I said.' I nodded and turned towards the door.

Jock frowned. 'What did you say that needs re-membering?'

Eva smiled faintly and shook her head as she dozed off. And Jock, who had never talked to me about anything that mattered, was unable to do so now.

As he drove me back to the house he said, 'Don't come again. You wore her out.' I packed my few things the next day, ready to return to school as soon as Mrs Fisher appeared. She made me have a bowl of soup with her and then ordered a cab to take me to the station. While we were waiting she said, 'I'm only here because of her, you know. He's a wicked, wicked man. I never knew she had a daughter till the question of my holidays came up. She's frightened of him, but I'll look after her, don't you worry. That's if she comes out of that place. If she's got any sense she'll give up now. I tell you, I'd rather die than live with him.'

The taxi arrived before I could ask her what she meant,

and I was glad because I didn't want to know. I gave the dogs a big hug and they licked my face until it was all wet. Then Mrs Fisher gave me a big kiss too and it was nearly as wet as the dogs' had been. I was very confused.

I rang the solicitor that evening from the school secretary's office. He was vague, brief, distant. 'I'll send you all the relevant papers, but you must sign them in front of a reliable witness.'

'Will my headmistress do?'

'Yes, that'll be all right. She's a Dame isn't she?'

'Er, yes. What are the papers about?'

'This flat of your mother's. She wants you to have it. She used to let it sometimes but it's empty now. You'll need somewhere to go when you leave school. Your stepfather doesn't know about the flat, and he mustn't until the papers are signed. So sign them and send them back immediately. If she dies before that we're in trouble: he'll find out and contest it. I've had an inventory done. Two teaspoons missing but I didn't want to worry your mother with that. Haste is essential. Understand? Essential.' He hung up.

I sat down, not knowing what anyone was talking about, as though the world had gone mad but forgotten to tell me. The headmistress came out of her study but I didn't notice at first and therefore failed to stand up. Her nickname was Dame Divine.

'Sadie Thompson, your bottom was given to you to hold your legs to your back. When that function is exhausted then its subsidiary function as a cushion may be employed. Your mother's husband has telephoned to request you not to visit her again. You were too boisterous. You wore her out.'

I stood up. 'Is my mother going to die?'

'Die? Of course not. You know that. The cessation of breath merely means that the next journey, to Purgatory, may begin. Only the truly wicked are sent to eternal damnation. Your mother's Purgatory, I'm sure, will be a time of preparation and excitement.'

'Is she going to die?'

'Death does not exist.'

'Is she, then, about to begin further travels? To Purgatory, for example?'

'Cancer does sometimes have that effect. But she will not suffer unless she has sinned.'

I walked past her open mouth and the open door towards the playing fields. The secretary followed me.

'Sadie, I couldn't help hearing that. I wish I could say take no notice, but I can't, so I won't. But do remember, she's quite, quite crazy. It's only because the board are crazier that she's still here. She used to be fantastic, before she got God. The bell will go in a minute. Shall we have a cup of coffee and talk about your mum?'

I frowned and shook my head frantically. 'Thank you. But no.'

'Another time then? Later? You say when. I'll be here.'

I shook my head again, but politely.

'Thanks, but I know how busy you are. If I could ring the hospital from your telephone later? And another thing: I've got some solicitor's papers to sign. When they come, could you help me with them?'

'Of course. Any time. And if you do want to talk about, you know . . . '

'No. If she's going to die then it's much, much too late.'

'It's never too late.'

But it was. I never saw my mother alive again although she didn't actually die for another month, the day after my nineteenth birthday.

Three

The papers from the solicitor arrived promptly and Rosie, the school secretary, helped me sort them out as she had promised.

Apparently my mother had owned the flat in Seymour Street for years although she hadn't lived there herself since the first of her three marriages. There had been a series of tenants and the accumulated rent money had been looked after by trustees on my behalf. I wasn't rich, but there was enough to keep me ticking over for a bit. I was amazed that after all those years of giving me nothing emotionally she had nevertheless thought of me enough to give me some financial security.

The last three weeks of term passed as usual, only now each day was punctuated by my telephone calls to the hospital. The answer was always the same: no change.

I minded very much about my A levels, especially as I had done well in my mocks, but the prospect of security softened the blow. Education had never been the school's forte anyway, so I didn't get much sympathy except from Rosie and meanwhile I concentrated on the extra-curricular activities that Dame Divine was so proud of. Endless flower arranging. Planning dinner party menus. Deportment. Etiquette. Cocktail party chit-chat. Vegetable and herb gardening. And the one thing I really enjoyed: driving. I had passed my test months before and

I used to break the rules and get up early to drive along the country lanes whilst they were still blurry with mist.

Then came the end of term and I packed up all my belongings and was driven to the station in the school bus. I had the key to the flat and enough money for a taxi the other end. There was some money waiting for me in Seymour Street and after that it would come in monthly instalments. Turning the key in the lock was one of the most extraordinary moments of my life. It was me, Sadie Thompson, versus the rest of the world. I was excited, curious and not at all frightened. I was responsible to absolutely no one.

Inside, the flat was small, but compact, two rooms, kitchen and bathroom, all opening off a central window-less corridor. The furniture was early G-Plan, which in a way was ideal. I could stamp my own imprint on it, as soon as I found what my imprint was. I unpacked my few things and then walked around just touching the walls until it was time to phone the hospital. First of all I talked to a nurse who said, 'As well as can be expected'. Then I heard Sister in the background, asking who it was and on being told my name she took the receiver herself.

'Miss Thompson? Your mother is less well. In fact she is unconscious. I'm sorry.'

'Thank you. May I come and see her?'

'It's such a long journey for you and she won't recognise you, I promise you.'

'That doesn't matter.' She had never recognised me in my life except for my one short visit to her in that same hospital. 'Please may I come?'

'If it was just up to me I'd say yes, my dear. But your stepfather remains adamant.'

'He's not my stepfather. He's my mother's husband.'

'Stay by the phone. I will ring you the minute there's any change.'

'When she comes round you mean?'

'I said any change. You must be prepared for bad news, Miss Thompson. Be prepared.'

I was never in the Boy Scouts so I said, 'Look, I must sound stupid but I don't understand your euphemisms. Any change. Be prepared. What exactly do you mean?'

'Ummmm. How old are you?'

'Nineteen yesterday.'

'You sound younger.'

'Curiosity isn't a prerogative of old age.'

'I'm sorry. You're right. I'll tell you but you mustn't come and see her. It would upset you too much. When I said be prepared for any change, what I meant was be ready for her to die.'

'Die? She can't die. We have some unfinished business. She won't die until she sees me. I know she won't.'

'Hang on a minute, love. Yes, Nurse?'

I heard her hand covering the mouthpiece of her phone. Her palm must have been very slippery because I could hear a slightly damp, squeaky noise. Then there was a longer, quieter silence. My head seemed full of candy floss. The silence continued, stretching between the two telephones.

Then, 'Miss Thompson? Are you there?'

'Yes,' I said, honestly.

'Miss Thompson, I'm very sorry. Your mother died approximately three minutes ago. It was quite painless.' And 'Who for? Who for?' I wanted to scream.

'Thank you, Sister. Goodbye.'

'Miss Thompson . . .'

I hung up. I felt detached, uninvolved, unaware how long it was going to take before I could live with my guilt; my mother's guilt.

I sat for some time then I got up and started searching the flat violently for clues of my mother's existence. I lifted carpets, moved furniture, pulled up floorboards, half hoping I'd find a letter addressed to 'my beloved daughter' or at least a scrap of paper in her handwriting, something on it to prove she had existed. Nothing. Too many houseproud tenants coming and going. I went out and did some shopping, wondering whether, years ago, my mother had used these same shops. But they were all supermarkets now, run by fresh-faced schoolboys and girls.

Back in the flat I made some tea, moved the furniture around a bit and sorted out my books. I'd bought some flowers and a couple of plants and as I sipped my tea I reflected that it was possible I would be more comfortable now than I ever had been in my mother's lifetime. It was dark and the lights were on and the flat seemed quite cosy. I read for a while and then got ready for bed. It was a double bed and I found myself wondering as I got into it if my mother had ever shared it with anyone, if perhaps, I might even have been conceived here. How disgusted she would have been by that thought.

The next day I spent writing to publishing houses to see if they had any vacancies for readers or even proof readers, quoting my high grades in the mock English exams as though they were the true results. When I went out to post the letters I bought some fabric and a couple of prints in a junk shop and spent the rest of the day making curtains and cushion covers.

It was only on the following day that I dared to buy a copy of *The Times*. I waited until I got home before I looked through the deaths column and then I could no longer pretend that it hadn't happened. The funeral was in two days' time, at the church in the Cotswold village near the hospital.

It was a long journey and I set off early in the morning. I didn't go to the house first but straight to the church, which appeared to be carved from one piece of the beautiful golden grey Cotswold stone. It was a very hot day and the coolness in the church was at first welcoming and then oppressive, so I went out again and wandered around the graveyard. I stood for a few moments by the freshly dug grave that was obviously destined for Eva. The damp earth smelled good and I threw a few wild flowers into the hole. Then I heard the sound of the hearse and saw people walking towards me and I hurried back into the church and sat in the back row with my head bent. The priest spoke very quietly and I was the only person who joined in the responses.

He did the full Ashes to Ashes bit and then it was time to follow the coffin out to its womb in the ground. There were perhaps twenty people there and of those twenty I recognised only Jock and Mrs Fisher. The heavy noise of earth on wood and already people were turning away, anxious to get back to the party.

I would have left straight away but Mrs Fisher saw me and latched on to my arm and guided me back to the house. 'He said you weren't coming, but I knew you'd get here somehow. We should have buried him instead. He's a wicked man. I have something for you that your mother asked me to give you.'

Her grip on my arm was strong and it would have been brutal to shrug her off. Inside, the house was prepared as for a party, tables groaning with food and drink, but mostly with drink. People I had never seen before were weeping noisily so that for a brief moment I thought that I must have come on the wrong day, to the wrong funeral. It was not improbable that Jock was letting the house out already for funeral receptions, since it was so near the church. His money-making ideas were always inspired by things that had happened to him, not by any scientific calculation. I had once pretended to myself that he'd set up a company for step-parents to swop stories. They'd have monthly dinners, rather like Freemasons, with a trouser leg rolled up and tee shirts printed 'These kids are not mine' and badges that said 'It was a job lot'.

Jock, playing the genial host, suddenly saw me as he was pouring drinks for everyone and his face darkened and the whisky overflowed on to the cucumber sandwiches. If Mrs Fisher had not been holding my arm I don't quite know what would have happened. The general weeping had now turned to raucous sobbing and the beginning of vulgar reminiscences, and Mrs Fisher and I left the room. I went upstairs with her and she produced a package wrapped in newspaper. I opened it and it was a carved mahogany Mother and Child that I had seen on the wall wherever my mother had lived. I remembered that perfect curve from long, long before I re-met my mother with Jock.

'Don't let him see it. Put it in your bag. Your mother wanted you to have it, she told me so, when she had to go into hospital. She made me promise to give it to you. It goes with the flat, she said. I don't know what she meant by that, perhaps you do, but I've kept my promise.'

I kissed her, her brown face seamed with tears, so that they brushed off on me and she stood back and wiped my face with a handkerchief saying, 'Don't cry, child, don't cry.' I put the package in my bag. 'Thank you, Mrs Fisher. Thank you. I must go now. I don't belong here. But can I just see the dogs before I go?'

She started weeping again, pulling me close to her so that once more my face was as wet as hers. Without letting go of me she said into my hair, 'I told you he was wicked, but that's not the right word, not strong enough. He had them put down the day your mother died. He had them killed.'

I pushed her away to look at her face, no longer

pretending my tears were really hers. 'He did what?'

'You heard me right. He murdered them. Just like he murdered your mother with coldness. He won't see me again. I helped get all this ready but I won't be here to clear up for him. Not now that I know that. He told me just before we left to go to the church.'

Her honest face was out of place in this house. 'You go too, Sadie. He's jealous of you. Go now.'

'Thank you for everything, Mrs Fisher. I'm glad Eva . . . my mother . . . had someone like you near her. Can you ring for a taxi for me?'

Mrs Fisher looked at me. 'Can you drive?' I nodded my head. 'In that case why bother with a taxi? He's got three cars out there. Nobody needs three cars. Here,' and she fumbled in her pocket and produced a set of keys. 'Here you are. He'll be so drunk by now he won't notice. Won't notice till tomorrow at the earliest. I won't be coming back. You won't see him again. All square, eh?'

We giggled like naughty schoolgirls and went into the bathroom. She locked the door behind us and stood leaning against the key whilst I went to the loo and washed my face and hands. My reflection in the mirror looked back at me as though nothing had happened. She was grinning now, pleased with herself and a little frightened of her own daring.

'Which car do the keys fit, do you know?'

'The new one. Dark blue. I think they call it a Mercedes?'

'The Mercedes?' Now I was slightly shocked.

'Yes. I chose that because it's got what I think they call comprehensive insurance. I know it means anyone can drive it because he gets drunk so often people are always having to drive him home. And I've got the log book and all the bits of paper I think you need. My Ted came up here last night and sorted it all out. He thought it was a very good idea. I said to him, "That poor girl's going to come all this way, how else will she get home?" And he said, "I see what you mean, gal. How is she going to get home?" He's a good man, my Ted. Never done a bad thing in all his life. So, if he thinks it's all right, it's all right.'

There was drunken singing from downstairs now and someone was playing the piano. Nervousness made me have another pee and as I pulled my knickers up I said, 'Well, if your Ted reckons it's all right, I guess it must be.'

She put the packet of car papers in my bag and handed me the keys. 'O.K.? Get going, girl. Soon as you've gone I'm off too. Look after yourself. You're the image of your mother. Don't make her mistakes. Have her happiness for her. I'll go first, make sure the coast is clear.'

I followed her down the stairs, back in the hockey goal with no pads.

She gave me a big kiss and opened the front door. The singing and laughing were even noisier close to but nevertheless my footsteps on the gravel drive sounded terribly loud and scrunchy. I got into the car, which was luckily facing the right way, gave Mrs Fisher a brief thumbs up sign and drove off into the lowering sun.

Four

I drove through the village carefully, getting the feel of the car, along the lanes where I used to walk the dogs, not terribly sure where I was. Then the roads became wider and I began to see signs to the motorway. The car was automatic and that increased my contempt for Jock. Real men knew how to change gear. The car smelled of Arpège. My mother had always hated Arpège. So it hadn't taken him long, then. Four days. Not bad going. A less expensive smell would have hurt less.

As I neared the motorway I passed several hitch-hikers and company suddenly seemed a good idea. I stopped at the next person I saw with a placard saying London.

I opened the door. The man gave me a funny look, as he said, 'Thought you'd be older. This car. You shouldn't really do this, you know. Too dangerous. I'm Tim.' He climbed in, put his bag on the back seat and slammed the passenger door shut. 'You could get raped. I'll give you petrol money. Think of that. Rape. In this car. They'd have to think of a more luxurious name for it. Never stop again. I'm O.K., I've got the clap, and I'm pretty selfish, I'm going to keep it all to myself.'

'My name is Sadie.'

'Are you all right? You look . . . .'

'Don't tell me. I've just been to a funeral, but we were

29

there for different people. I feel stupid. And sad. And guilty. And foolish. Bayswater O.K.?'

We hit the motorway and drove in silence. Tim laughed a couple of times. I took no notice. The first time I overtook a Porsche and the second time I looked at the petrol gauge. The bastard hadn't even left me a full tank. 'We'll have to stop at the next service station. Get your money ready. This car runs on Glenfiddich. Four star.'

I eased into the inside lane, loathing the car, its smoothness, its silence, the scent my mother hated.

As we walked towards the cafeteria I looked back at the car and finally felt extremely pleased with myself. The sense of triumph that had been missing when I had stolen Jock's money all those years ago was finally mine. Even he would notice that one of his cars was gone when he sobered up in the morning. I wasn't sure I could wait until then.

We blinked as we entered the brightly lit building and looked each other up and down, finally seeing who we were. I liked what I saw. He didn't appear disappointed. Tim was taller than me and that redressed the imbalance of me in that ridiculous car. We smiled at each other. My mouth straightened first and Tim said, 'Sorry, I can't stop smiling. It's just so nice to see your face in the light and not be disappointed. What would you like to eat?'

'Nothing, thanks. But a big cup of coffee would be O.K.'

He was still smiling; he had a look I had never seen directed at me before and I felt afraid and happy at the same time.

The car seemed less important and I wanted to get it out of the way now so that I could concentrate on Tim.

'I'll see you in a minute, Tim. I've just got to make a phone call. Don't go away . . .'

I went to the row of telephones outside but there was a

queue so I went to the lavatory first. While I was drying my hands under the hot air machine that takes so much longer than paper towels, I looked in the mirror. I still didn't look like someone who had been to a funeral. A christening, perhaps. Possibly my own.

There was an empty phone box now and I felt a tremor of fear as I heard the number ringing but when the receiver was picked up, before anyone spoke I heard music and laughter, and after that it was easy. Jock's voice was slurred with alcohol and he couldn't say the number properly. I made him get it right before I spoke.

'This is Sadie. I've taken one of your cars. The one smelling of Arpège. Eva hated Arpège. And anyway, it's not a good car for pulling, you must have just struck lucky. Women with style think Mercedes are vulgar and automatics unmanly, so really I'm doing you a favour. I think I've got all the relevant papers, so if we hear no more from each other we can consider the account is closed. If you try to get it back I'll have to contact a lawyer about the will you've mislaid. Those fights always get reported in the papers, even the *Financial Times*. R.I.P., Daddy dear.' And then the pips went and I hung up.

Tim looked miserable when I returned.

'What's the matter?' I said, helping myself to some of his chips with an intimacy that appeared to delight him.

'Nothing. You just look so happy you must have been talking to a lover.'

I blushed. 'If only you knew. Anyway, I should be so lucky. And even if I had been you shouldn't look so sad. I thought everybody loved a lover.'

His smile was nearly back. 'I guess so. I just forgot the tune for a minute.'

'That's one of the great tragedies in my life, that I can't sing. I can hear it perfectly in my head but it seems to come out of my mouth like a scrambler. Hmm. Good coffee. More?'

He nodded and put his last chip in my mouth. The second cup of coffee might have been dishwater but it tasted good. Tim asked me about my parents and it seemed churlish to say nothing. 'My mother died giving birth to me and I never knew my father. You?'

'Oh, middle-aged, middle class, feeling cheated because they missed out on the nuclear family seal of respectability.'

'2·4 kids?'

'I can never work that out, the ·4 bit.'

'No, but it's divisible by two which makes it easier for the Civil Service. What do you do?'

'It never quite sounds true when I say it but I'm a deep-sea diver. I'm working in the North Sea at the moment, but I've spent some time in the Gulf and I'd like to go back there one day.' And then for some reason he added, 'But not yet.'

I felt ridiculously pleased, and then he said, 'Where do you live?'

'Near where I'm dropping you off. How about you?'

'Oh, when I'm in London I stay in the house I lived in when I was a student – it's kind of been handed down from student to student and I pay a retainer so I always have somewhere to crash when I'm down. Notting Hill.'

'No car?'

'Not any more. I used to have one when I was a student – used to minicab in it when I was broke – terrible old banger it was too. But it had four doors. That's the only prerequisite for minicabbing. Then I left it in London at the house, so not only did I have a bed, I also had transport. Used to, till last week.'

'What happened then?'

'Someone nicked it, didn't think too much of it and

left it at the end of the road, first removing the only bits of it that were any good.'

'Four doors? So that's why you're hitching?'

'Yeah. Too old really. It's O.K. when you're twenty-nine, but when you're pushing thirty . . . But I had to go home today because it was my mother's birthday and she gets a bit sniffy if I don't go and see her. And it makes life easier for Dad. You're very beautiful.'

I thought he was taking the piss but when I looked at him I could see he wasn't. He, too, was beautiful, and for the first time in my life I understood the meaning of 'I want', and I could see that he felt it too. Only not for the first time.

We got back in the car and drove round to the filling station. Tim paid for the petrol and I let him.

As we drove over the Westway towards Bayswater Tim asked me for my telephone number.

'I have never,' I said primly, 'given my telephone number or address to a known carrier of venereal disease.'

'In that case,' said Tim, 'I'll have to give you mine. But I'm only here for four more days and then I'm away in Scotland for nearly two weeks.'

He took an envelope out of his pocket, removed the contents and wrote his address and phone number on the back.

'That's a bit silly, isn't it?' I said. 'Surely it's already there, on the front?'

'I wanted to save you the bother of having to turn it over. That might give you time to change your mind.'

'Ah. Time and motion study. How clever.'

I stopped the car on the corner of Albion Street and Bayswater Road.

'Please let me have your phone number. I've nearly finished my course of penicillin. Tomorrow in fact. Please give me your number or address.'

33

More than anything I wanted to give them to him but I couldn't remember the telephone number and giving him just the address seemed a bit fast, as Dame Divine would have said. Instead I opened my bag and took out the envelope containing the log book and the insurance cover, all the bits Mrs Fisher's husband had considered relevant. I left the keys in the car and handed him the package, opening the driver's door as I spoke. 'Here. Have the car. It's harder to lose than a telephone number. Be a berk with a Merc. But you'll have to extend the penicillin course; I understand this is a good pulling car. It's just that I can't bear being in it a minute longer. There are other kinds of funerals.'

I slammed the driver's door behind me and hailed a passing taxi, which pulled in just in front of Tim. I ran to the cab and told him my destination and then as I was climbing in I suddenly ran back to Tim and said, 'Bye. Thanks for the lift. And don't take it personally. I want you. But I'm a virgin and I'd be a terrible disappointment to you.'

And then I was again in the safe and sexless anonymity of the black cab that was going to take me all of a hundred yards.

Five

Back in the flat, exhausted and confused by all sorts of miseries and emotions, I went straight into the bedroom and lay on the bed, numbness closing my eyes and then exhilaration forcing them open so that the wall in front had a kaleidoscopic appearance. At first it seemed that my eyes were playing tricks with me and that the faded wallpaper was taking on a life of its own and presenting me with a shape that was only in my imagination. I closed my eyes tightly and counted up to a hundred before opening them again very fast so that the paper didn't have time to play its tricks on me. The faded shape was quite, quite definitely there. I jumped off the bed and unwrapped the mahogany Madonna that Mrs Fisher had given me and held it up against the faded patch. It fitted perfectly. There was even the stub end of a nail sticking out for it to hang on. I tried to reach but I was not quite tall enough so I pulled a chair over and this time I managed to hang the plaque in place. I lay back on the bed again and gazed at it. I felt as though someone had shown me my birth certificate.

I lay on my side, pulling my knees up against my belly but with my head still turned so that I could see my Mother and Child. I felt real happiness, a belated sense of belonging that absolutely nothing and nobody could ever take away from me again.

In the bureau the envelope that Eva had given me was tucked into a secret compartment. Chris. I must ring Chris. As I dialled the number I realised that I had no idea whether it was a he or a she whom I was about to talk to. And even when the voice the other end said hello I wasn't quite sure.

'Hello. My name is Sadie Thompson.'

There was a silence that I felt I had to fill but didn't know how to.

'Eva's Sadie?'

'Eva's Sadie.'

There was a shorter silence then, 'And Eva?'

'She died five days ago.'

Her voice almost changed sex, became rougher, cracked. 'Oh God. Poor Eva. I tried to see her at first but that man would never let me. She must have been unhappy to let him get away with that. She was still with that ghastly brigadier fellow, was she?'

'Yes.'

Another silence.

'Her death. Did it hurt?'

'He only let me see her once. She looked very pale but didn't seem to be in pain.'

'Thank God. How did you get my number?'

'That one time I was allowed to see her, he went out and she gave me an envelope. Key and address of a flat. Solicitor's name. And your number. She wanted me to ring you when I moved into the flat but then she died. Her terminal bun fight is still going on I expect, with Jock as Master of Ceremonies.'

Silence again and then I continued, 'I'm sorry if I've bothered you. It's just – she told me to – so I did. I'll hang up now.'

'Wait, wait, don't hang up. So you're Sadie.'

'Yes, I'm Sadie. Can I come and see you?'

'Of course you can. But not until next week. Not because I don't want to see you, I can't wait, but I have to go away for a few days. I can't get out of it now, but after that any time you want me I'm here and I'm yours.'

'Really?'

'I promise you.'

'When shall I ring you then?'

'Oh, no. I'm not taking any chances like that. You might forget. Give me your number and I'll ring you the very minute I'm back.'

'It's 723 . . . '

'Oh, you're in her flat? I've got the number.'

'How on earth do you know it?'

'I've known Eva forty-odd years. Look, I have to go now, I've got someone with me, but I'll ring you the minute I walk in the door. You have no idea how much we have to talk about. It's so wonderful, hearing your voice. I want to celebrate, grieve. But Eva – beautiful Eva – just give me a couple of days alone, to absorb what you've told me and to remember. I'll ring you the minute I get home. You have me now. O.K.? Don't forget that. See you next week. Oh – Eva's Sadie. I can hardly believe it. 'Bye Sadie.'

I went back into the bedroom and lay fully dressed on the bed staring at that beautiful simple object that had changed my life. The room darkened around us and when I could no longer see it I fell asleep.

The next morning it was the first thing I saw and I couldn't stop smiling. I went shopping early, snooping round junk shops, and then spent the rest of the day beginning to make the flat into my home. I had three replies from publishers, two nos and one would I like to go and see them. I rang and made an appointment for the following day. My record player was now working so I had music and books and flowers all around me. I spent

37

most of the day smiling. I thought of Tim a few times too, and then I stopped smiling and wished I had given him my phone number and wondered about the car, how he was getting on with it, whether he could afford the petrol for it, feeling ambiguous about giving something away that meant nothing to someone who meant something.

The next day I bathed and washed my hair early and wondered what to wear to try and look literary. I couldn't think of anything so wore my usual dungarees but added a pair of those sunglasses that are supposed to go dark in the sun, safe in the knowledge that it was pouring with rain, and headed off towards Bloomsbury.

The girl who interviewed me was very nice and gave me some proofs to take home, saying that if I did well and spotted enough mistakes the job was mine. Things were going almost too well. Back home I read a couple of the books and worried because I could find hardly any mistakes, so I decided to go out for a walk or maybe go to a film. The hot summer weather of my mother's funeral had evaporated and it was wet and windy that night as I walked round the corner into Edgware Road and tagged cosily on to the end of a shivering bus queue, for the cold and damp hadn't permeated me yet.

I was staring at the headlights coming towards me, blurred and curiously comforting, like knowing you're on the right runway even if you are about to crash.

I was aware of the darkness of the back of the head in front of me reversing itself briefly into a pale image of its shadow. Then back to darkness again and there was a moment when the traffic seemed to be going at an insane, ridiculous speed. Another moment and then the world's lights seemed to fuse and the only thing left that wasn't dark and frightening was Tim's face turning back towards me.

'Thanks for the lift,' he said and the master switch flicked on.

My control over my face deserted me and I smiled with delight.

'Tim.'

'Sadie.'

That was one of the best moments of my life.

'Drink?' he said, guiding me into the pub next to the bus stop. 'Glenfiddich?'

And we both laughed as the pub doors closed behind us.

'Actually,' I said, 'I'd love a drink and lime juice would be great.'

'In this weather? I think a whisky mac would do you more good.'

'If you say so.'

As we sipped our drinks Tim said, '*Now* will you tell me where you live? I've spent two days looking for you. I tried to follow the cab but the bastard jumped the lights.'

'About thirty yards from here, where the cab jumped the light. I don't go out much. Don't talk to any strange men, they said. So I don't.'

'Trouble is, she knows them all.'

I blushed with innocence, demanding recognition. 'You're wrong. So wrong.'

'Good. I'm glad. And sorry I said that. But very glad I am so wrong.'

And now our smiles and silences could lead only to the relief of honesty, it seemed. I wanted to be totally truthful with Tim and I paused, searching for the words to correct the lie I had told him about my mother. But I left it a moment too long and Tim spoke first. 'So much to say. I can't imagine how awful it must be to have no parents, but mine are smashing, so why don't you

39

consider them yours? Surrogate parents. O.K.?' And so I was exiled for ever with my mother's dead body. And then he made it worse by adding, 'I've felt so many things about you since I saw you, but most of all I've remembered the loneliness in your voice when you said your mother died when you were born. That's haunted me. I may be mean about my parents but they were always there with the odd fiver when I was a student.'

I tried to say Tim, I'm sorry I told you a lie but I didn't know you were going to matter so much when we touched for the first time. Frightened out of my wits I went to the loo. I was bleeding, paying my dues for being a woman. My heart went out to Tim when I saw how nervous he looked, how very far from complacent. One little white lie between lovers, for we would become lovers, that's all Eva was now.

Tim saw me returning and the reassurance came from me, my smile, for the first time. Another drink. No need to hurry now. Everything under control.

'Cheers,' I said as I put the drinks down on the wobbly table.

'Cheers,' said Tim. 'Where were you going tonight? Was someone waiting?'

'Only Godot's lot. I was going to see a movie, if a bus had come. If not, I was going for a walk, to get some fresh air. Well, air.'

'You convent girls. Going for walks in the pouring rain.'

'How did you know I went to . . . '

'People like you always do. Sign of the times.'

'Not the Cross?'

'*Times* crossword?'

'Why are you talking such rubbish?'

'Sometimes,' Tim said carefully, 'it's the safest thing to talk, rubbish.'

As we left the pub an all-night dustcart rumbled past, splashing the gutter water in a fine, accurate, saturating catamaran-helm spray. We stood there, soaking wet and laughing.

'That's what comes of talking rubbish,' I said.

'If only I knew someone who lived near here,' said Tim, 'we could go and get dry.'

'But I live alone. I've only just moved here. And no one has ever been home with me before. I live alone . . .'

I didn't get very far. 'Sure you live alone. You still do. I'm wet, is all. Not moving in. Just drying out.'

'Well you'll have to wait downstairs while I see if it's tidy.'

'Oh no. You're not disappearing again. I'm not losing you now. I'll look the other way while you tidy up if you like. Anyway, how can one person be untidy?'

We were outside my front door now, on the first floor. As I turned the key in the lock I said, 'O.K., now I'm not going to run away, but please wait here while I check that everything is decent. Please?'

'O.K. But if you haven't finished by the time I count to twenty I'm coming in anyway.'

I pushed the door of the sitting room open and quickly closed it behind me. The room could never have been called untidy but there were some bits of washing drying on a clothes horse and it was those clothes that I wanted to move. Even now I was embarrassed at the thought of anyone seeing my underwear. I scooped up several very small pairs of knickers and a flimsy nightdress, rolled them up and stuffed them under a cushion, blushing as though I had turned up to make a speech for the Festival of Light stark naked. I lit the gas fire and crouched down very near it, too near it, so that the redness of my face could if necessary be attributed to my proximity to the flames.

And outside in the hall Tim was chanting, 'Sixteen, seventeen, eighteen, nineteen . . . '

'Save the twenty for another time. Come in. Sit down, take your wet things off. I'll go and get you a towel,' and I went off towards the door on the other side of the hall.

Safely in the bathroom, I took a Tampax out of the cupboard fast, as though it were a tourniquet. Then I scooped up all the towels, draped one of them over my wet head and took the others in to Tim. He was crouching in front of the fire, trying to get warm. He was stark naked and his skin appeared to be steaming slightly. I threw him the towels and turned my back, terrified of what I might see.

Then I half turned towards him but as though I had no eyes so that my 'Coffee?' sounded curiously blind. The sight of the towels, one round his head and the other, more important, round his waist, restored both my vision and my composure and I was able to say 'Coffee?' as if I really meant it this time.

'In a minute,' said Tim as though I had spoken in church, 'in a minute. You must get dry first, you're soaked to the skin. I think you should take all your clothes off.'

There was a pause and then he started to walk towards me. I couldn't move for a moment, torn between wanting his hands on me, helping me off with my soaking wet clothes, and the memory of Eva's voice telling me that being a woman was dirty, Jock folding the *Financial Times* neatly open to study his stocks and shares, the stale smell of his small single bed. If I left it much longer I'd be dry anyway and besides I hadn't known Tim long enough; he probably felt he owed me something for the car. If I hadn't just started my period and offered him coffee perhaps it would have been different.

I edged towards the door. 'Right. Yes. You're quite

right. I should take my clothes off. It's very kind of you to think of me. I'll just go and do that. Thank you very much.'

As I closed the door behind me I was shaking with a mixture of anger, relief and frustration. I went into the bathroom and stripped and towelled myself so fiercely dry that my whole body appeared to be blushing, only for the wrong reason. I went through into the bedroom and put on old towelling robe. I didn't want to make him feel underdressed. Then I made coffee and took it in, my hands shaking a bit so that it spilled on the tray, hoping that he wouldn't be angry with me. Someone at school had once told me that there was nothing more irritating than a reluctant virgin. And I wasn't sure whether or not he knew quite how unreluctant I was.

I was glad that I hadn't dressed up since he was still clad only in my towels. I made a private resolve to buy bigger towels as soon as I had enough money. The coffee was foul, instant and I hadn't quite let the kettle boil, afraid that he might have come looking for me, so there were little blobs of powder in it. His clothes were steaming slightly in front of the fire and I wished I had a spin dryer so that neither of us would have to prolong this agony. However, when I finally looked at him, he seemed perfectly at ease, stretched out like some contented gladiator who had just been told that the lion to whom he was to be thrown had toothache.

He drank the coffee as though it was actually rather good and finally we found ourselves talking as though nothing had happened. Which in a sense was true. I sat as far away from him as I could while he regaled me with anecdotes about his student days and I envied him the camaraderie that he seemed to take for granted. Then he talked a bit about his job and I found that less pleasant. It seemed dangerous and lonely and boring by turns and I didn't want to know about that side of his life.

The only drink in the house was some vile sweet sherry that must have been left behind by the last tenants. We managed to drink it, however, and by the time we had finished it two things had happened. One was that I felt rather drunk, and the other was that his clothes were no longer steaming. I yawned. Not because I wanted him to go but because I was once again afraid of my own feelings. He looked at me for a moment.

'Well, I suppose I'd better be going,' he said and stretched so hard that the towel was in danger of coming apart at a crucial place.

I stood up quickly. 'I'll just take the coffee things out,' I said like a waitress anticipating a generous tip for efficient service.

I managed to get them to the kitchen without dropping anything and then spent a long time not only washing them up but also drying them and putting them away, something I normally never did.

I banged around a bit on my way back and coughed rather stupidly as I opened the door. He was in exactly the same position as before but this time he was fully dressed and it was the towels that were steaming slightly in front of the fire.

'Sadie, I have to go to work very early the day after tomorrow, and I have to spend the day at head office, so I won't see you until I get back in about ten days' time. May I ring you? I'm not going to lose you again.'

I shrugged. 'It's up to you.'

'And you,' said Tim. 'You're in my head. You know that, don't you?'

I looked at the carpet and shrugged again.

'Well, you are. And you know it. But we've got lots of time. I'll be with you again very soon. Wait for me, Sadie?'

And then I had to look at him. It hurt and it must have shown, for he leaned forward and kissed me very gently. I trembled slightly.

He touched my face with the back of his hand, and I shivered again.

'I know. It's the same for me. I'll see you soon.'

And then he was gone, because I watched him walk out of the door. And yet everywhere I looked I saw him.

It took me a long time to get to sleep that night.

Six

The two days after Tim left and before Chris rang seemed very long indeed. Even the little mahogany Madonna failed to give me the comfort that it had once before. It still warmed me when I looked at it but there was now something missing, something indefinable that I failed to understand entirely. Tim rang me once from Scotland but his voice was very faint. He was just about to go out to the rig I think, but he said that he would write to me and that he would see me very soon. I said 'Good', which didn't sound very enthusiastic but I had never found it easy to show emotion about things that mattered.

The following evening the phone rang again. I was in bed, nearly asleep and my 'Hello' was sleepy until I heard Chris's bright voice.

'Hello, my darling girl. I told you I'd wake you up as soon as I got back. Well I probably didn't say wake you up, but I should have done because I'm very much a night-time person. I don't like all this daytime do you?'

'Ummm. Never really thought about it. S'pose I don't really. It does go on a bit, doesn't it?'

Chris laughed. 'That's my girl. Now, it's half-past ten. Too late for you to come over?'

I was already out of bed. 'Not at all. What's your address?'

'Thirty-four Stanhope Crescent. Ground floor flat.'

'Right. I'll be with you as soon as I can. 'Bye.'

''Bye. See you soon.'

I got up quickly and dressed, combed my hair and was out hailing a taxi in Edgware Road in about five minutes flat.

Chris must have been waiting, for the door was opened before I had finished paying the cab driver and I was up the few steps and being wrapped in a bear-like hug almost before I knew what was happening.

'Come in, come in. There's gin or gin or tea or gin. I'm having gin and I think you should too. To celebrate.'

I smiled agreement and looked around the room. The flat was similar to mine. The layout was exactly the same but it was bigger; and there the similarities ended. This was a flat that had been lived in and loved for years.

The gin was very strong and as we sat down and said 'Cheers', Chris said, 'Look. You're Sadie and I'm Chris and that's what matters. I'm just going to ask you a couple of questions about Eva and then we, you and I, take it from there. O.K.?'

I nodded my head, hoping I would be able to answer her questions, for I knew so little of Eva. I took a large swallow of gin and nearly choked. Chris patted my back. 'No hurry, my lovely.'

She offered me one of her cigarettes, but they were untipped Woodbines, and as I had only just started smoking, I declined, telling her why. She immediately got up and went to a corner cupboard and produced some cocktail coloured Sobranies and some Rothmans. 'I always keep a few up-market ones as well. Some of my clients prefer them. Now tell me. What did Eva die of?'

'Cancer,' I said, lighting my cigarette.

'Oh God. That poor girl. Where did she have it?'

'Breast first. Then spine.'

'Much pain?'

'I'm not sure. As I told you on the phone, I was only allowed to see her once in hospital. The only thing I do know is that she was unconscious for the last few days. But she must have known she was going to die because she'd signed all the papers for the flat, making it over to me. She said Jock must never know about it.'

'Was she happy? With him?'

'Perhaps for a short time, but I think only a very short time. I didn't see them often. I was at boarding school mostly.'

'Was she good to you? Did she love you?'

'Not so's you'd notice. I tried very hard, but I was never good enough for her. In the end I was afraid of them both. I mean, I was always afraid of him.'

'Who wasn't?'

'And in the end I was afraid of her too. I never dared speak unless I was spoken to first. The only time I felt we might have had a chance, the one time I thought I recognised something between us was the last time I saw her. And then he never let me see her again. I rang the hospital every day and every day I asked the Sister if I could go and see her, but she always said no, he had forbidden it. She was very nice, but I think she was probably afraid of him too.'

I didn't look at Chris, because I could hear her weeping quietly.

'And you know what the very worst thing of all is, Chris? She's dead and I haven't been able to cry.'

Chris blew her nose abruptly, aware of her unfair advantage. 'I think another little drink is called for, don't you? And then no more talk of Eva. Some day I'll tell you about her, but not yet. We've got all the time in the world.'

'You're the second person to tell me that in the last three days.'

'Who was the first? No, let me guess. A boyfriend?'

'I don't really know. I've never had a boyfriend before. But I think he might become one.'

'Do you fancy him? Do you get a pain in your belly when you're with him?'

'Yes, how did you know that?'

'Then he'll be a boyfriend. How did you meet him?'

I blushed at the memory of what I'd done, but it was impossible not to be honest with Chris. So I told her the story of the funeral, of Jock getting drunk even before we got to the church, of Mrs Fisher and the Madonna, of meeting Tim.

'Sadie, my darling Sadie, that is the best story I have heard for years. How did he find you again?'

'He walked around looking for me. He knew I lived quite near. Then quite by chance I stood behind him at a bus stop two days later.'

Chris was crying with laughter now. 'I don't know. A Mercedes between you and you meet at a bus stop.'

'He said if it had been an old Mini he could have done a bit of kerb crawling, but a brand new Mercedes made that tricky.'

Now I was laughing as well, with happiness, and with Chris's infectious cackle it would have been almost impossible not to.

'Where is he now?'

'On some North Sea oil rig. But he'll be back in a few days. He says he's not going to let me get away from him again. I very much want to go to bed with him, but I'm frightened of not being good at it so I might lose him. I don't know anything about sex. Eva couldn't ever talk about it, and anyway they had separate bedrooms.'

'Poor Eva. But listen, my darling, don't worry about not being very good at it. If you want each other, you have no problems. Something else takes over. It's been

49

one of the greatest joys of my life, fucking. In fact you'll
have to go soon, I've got a client coming in about twenty
minutes.'

I must have looked surprised, for she smiled her
wonderful smile again and said, 'Look, I'm forty-five, I'm
no great beauty and I don't want to live with anyone
now. I don't want to have to do someone's washing for
them or cook them a meal if I don't feel like it. I've got
three things going for me. Honesty, a sense of humour,
and a love of sex. Oh, and I'm discreet. Actually, I've got
four things going for me now, I've got you as well. By
the way, come here to my bedroom, I want to show you
something.' And she led the way to her bedroom, which
was done up in great style with screens and feathers and
dried flowers and a huge brass bed with a patchwork
quilt. But the thing that caught my eye almost as soon as
I entered the room was hanging on the wall above the top
of the bed. It was an identical mahogany Madonna to the
one Mrs Fisher had thrust into my hands the week before.

'We bought them together years ago. I'm so very, very
glad you've got hers. The car is funny, but this is
important.'

I felt very happy, not yet curious about Chris's and
Eva's links.

'Now I must tizzy myself up a bit. They're all high
class, my gentlemen. Doctors, lawyers, judges, that sort
of thing. Occasionally some I just fancy, but I never let
them pay. What's your young man's name?'

'Tim.'

'Well, when he's back I don't expect I'll see you. But
when he's away I want to see you every day. Or at least
talk to you. We can lead double lives. I like a bit of
excitement. And if you really care about him, let me give
you one bit of advice. Never, ever, tell him a lie. Do
anything else, but don't lie to him.'

'Too late Chris. I already have.'

'But you've only met him twice.'

'I know,' I said, suddenly miserable. 'But when we stopped for petrol and coffee on the motorway he asked me about my family. I was feeling so mixed up about Eva and all those people singing and the smell of Arpège that I said I never knew my father, and my mother died giving birth to me. And the next time we met I tried to put it right but he got in first. He said I had sounded so lonely that he wanted to offer me his own parents as a surrogate family. By then I wanted him and I thought if I told him it was a lie I'd lose him.'

'I see. In a funny sort of way it was a true lie. You can't tell him the truth now, but for God's sake don't tell him any more. Now buzz off. I love you. You've made me very, very happy. I'll ring you tomorrow. But not too early. O.K., my lovely girl? And remember you've got me now, so you're not alone, even if Tim doesn't work out. But I'm sure he will. There's a cab rank just down the road. Until tomorrow? Much love.' And she gave me another of her huge embraces and I walked off into the night wishing that I had had a mother like Chris but happy that I had found her anyway.

Seven

The next morning I awoke happier than I could ever remember being. My Madonna seemed to smile at me, or maybe it was simply one of those days when everyone seems to smile. There was no letter from Tim but I hadn't actually expected one. I did, however, have one letter from the trustees with a surprisingly large monthly cheque, which I immediately cashed. I spent most of the money on more things for the flat, concentrating more on the bedroom than I had before. Indeed, by the time I had finished it rather resembled Chris's luxurious den. I also bought some small lamps so that I didn't have to use the overhead lamps at all. One went on either side of the bed, pointing up at the ceiling, and the others I placed around the little sitting room. Then I spent money on lots of pretty, feminine underwear, small things in colours from pastel to dark brown and even, daringly, black. I innocently bought some nighties, not realising how little I'd need them. Pleased with myself, I went over to see Chris in the early evening, but did not stay long as she had a busy night ahead of her. It was as though we had known each other for years. We finished the bottle of gin we had begun the night before and I felt a little tipsy when I got out of the cab. As I opened the front door, I could hear the telephone ringing. My hello was slightly slurred and Tim sounded a bit annoyed. 'Where are you? I mean, where have you been? This is the third time I've rung.'

'I went to see a friend. We had a couple of drinks, that's all.'

'Male or female friend?'

'Female. I only have one male friend and that's you.' And then the drink made me add, 'I wish you were here. I think about you a lot. I want you.'

There was a long silence whilst Tim took this in. Then, 'Well, perhaps you should have a drink more often if it makes you say things like that. But it's not very fair of you when I'm such a long way away and can't do anything about it. I was really ringing to say that I'll be home the day after tomorrow. There's some problem up here and we can't get on with much work, so rather than sit around doing sweet F.A. I'm coming home. To see you. I miss you quite ridiculously. See you soon.' And then the line went dead.

I hardly slept that night and was up very early again. I had forgotten to buy any records and I had a moment of panic in the shop since I had no idea what music he liked, so I chose a huge collection, Marianne Faithfull's 'Broken English', the Kinks' 'Low Budget', Dylan's 'Live at the Budokan', Stones' and Beatles' classics and Satie and Rodriguez for good measure. I also bought a new stylus. I filled the flat with masses of flowers and as soon as I considered it reasonably late I went over to see Chris, bubbling with excitement and nerves. She looked very tired when she opened the door, but when she saw me her face lit up. 'Come in, my darling. Thank God it's you and I don't have to make an effort to be polite. Or active, come to that. I can see from your face that you've heard from him.'

'Yes, he rang me last night. He's coming home tomorrow, not next week. I'm thrilled to bits, but I'm also scared. Suppose I can't do it well enough? He is ten years older than me and much more experienced. He's even had V.D.'

Chris's tone was sharp now. 'How long ago? Has he had treatment for it? And has he been back for a check-up? And what was he doing telling you he'd got that? Bragging or complaining?'

'Oh, Chris, it wasn't like that. He was telling me off for giving him a lift. Said I should never do it again, I might get raped. He said I was lucky I picked him up because he'd got V.D. so I was quite safe. And the course finished two days later and he went back for a check-up the day before he went back to Scotland. Well, he didn't actually say that's where he was going, but reading between the lines . . . '

'Never read between the lines, my girl. Sometimes you read what isn't there. Before you do anything, you ask him outright. I like the sound of him, he sounds an ideal person to lose your virginity with, but I'll be very angry if he gives you the clap first time round. And you can tell him that from me.'

'Yes, teacher.'

'Apart from that my darling, lie back and enjoy it. Don't despair if you don't have an orgasm the first time. Virgins rarely do. And stop worrying about what you have to do. Touch him where you want to touch him. Let him know what you like him doing to you. Have a little drink beforehand if that will help you relax. Or smoke a bit of dope. I've got one old bishop who can't do a thing until he's had a joint. Then he's like Red Rum out at stud. I'm going to send you home soon with a bottle of gin and some Columbian Gold. I'll even give you some skins. O.K.?'

'But Chris, I've never rolled a joint in my life.'

'Very well then, I'll roll you a couple to be getting on

54

with. But watch me very carefully. I can't spend my time sitting here rolling joints for you so that you can have a good sex life. You shouldn't need them, but just in case . . . '

I watched her, fascinated. She looked like a little old man suddenly, and there was no denying her speed and efficiency. She rolled a third. 'We'll share this one now. There must be at least one thing you're going to do tomorrow that you've done before.'

She lit it, took a deep drag and passed it to me. I puffed at it rather half-heartedly and Chris said, 'No, no, no,' and told me to watch her carefully. 'Open your mouth a bit more and take in some air with it, then hold it down for as long as you can. Try again . . . that's much better.' When I finally exhaled I felt rather faint, but by the time I had got to the end of the joint, sharing it puff for puff with Chris, I was really giggly. I just couldn't stop laughing, and when I got up to go to the loo I kept bumping into things, which made both of us laugh more.

'Well, my girl, if you do as well as that in bed tomorrow night I'll feel really proud of you. The loo is the bit with a seat on it, not the big thing with two taps at the end.'

By the time I had got myself together it was much later than we had thought and Chris's first client was due to arrive. She packed me off with a bottle of gin, a couple of tonics and the two joints in a nearly empty Rothmans' packet. 'Enjoy yourself, my darling. I'll hear from you when I hear from you.'

I was still giggling when we opened the front door, to be confronted by torrential rain. I gaily waved goodbye, and staggered across the road. Not an empty taxi in sight, so I walked home, smiling at the rain and enjoying the feeling of my clothes clinging to my saturated body. I

55

had never been so aware of my body before and I wished that Tim was coming home tonight and not tomorrow. I left a small puddle of water outside the front door as I fumbled for my key, smiling dopily at the lock which seemed unwilling to accept my key any other but the right way up. Finally I got it in the right way and the first thing I heard was the telephone ringing. Laughing, I picked it up, expecting it to be Chris. But it was Tim. 'Where are you?' was all I could say. 'Just around the corner from you,' he said. 'I flew down. I'll be with you in two minutes.' 'Two minutes,' I repeated. 'Right. Two minutes.'

Actually it was about a minute and a half, and I was still waiting by the front door when he arrived. He, too, was dripping wet.

'Haven't we been in this movie before?' he said, putting his arms round me until the puddle around our feet threatened to become a lake. He closed the front door behind us at last and I felt a tiny bit nervous, just for a moment as he said, 'I think you should take all your clothes off.'

He was standing behind me now, his fingertips tracing a pattern on my breasts, so that I arched my back against him, pushing against the hardness in his trousers, not turning towards him in case he saw how much pleasure he was giving me.

He said it again, 'I think you should take your clothes off. If I do it, I won't ever be sure that you won't regret it. I'll help you, I'll undo your buttons, but you must do the rest.'

His fingers reached under my dungarees and undid the buttons of my blouse. I had never known more exactly the meaning of 'I want'. And yet as he opened my blouse and I felt the cold summer night against my body, the hall silently filled with the shadows of Eva and Jock and the nuns until there was no space left for me and Tim and my eagerness shrivelled to reluctance and fear. But I think Tim imagined that it was only the cold that was making me shiver. Then he turned me to face him and put his arms round me very tightly. 'It's all right. There's plenty of time. The rest of our lives.'

I felt him smile against my hair as he tried to control my trembling.

'There's no rush. We're lucky. We have the rest of our lives.'

He made it sound a very long time.

Then I was alone again, and for a moment I thought he had left me. I heard the sound of the bath running. It was one of those old baths that filled up very quickly, so that when he came back and took my hand and led me into the bathroom it was nearly full. He didn't say anything at all as he, after all, undressed me, not hurrying now as the room was full of steam and very hot. As he uncovered each part of me, he kissed me and suddenly I, who had never been naked before anyone, found myself feeling unashamed and not at all dirty. Then he undressed too, and we were both in the bath together. He soaped my body all over, tantalizing me by the lightness of his touch on my breasts, just brushing against them, when what I wanted him to do was hold them hard until I could feel my nipples swell. Indeed, I pushed them into his hands, but he just kept saying, 'Not yet, not yet.'

Then he stood up and helped me out and dried me all over until my skin glowed and burned and I wanted to take it off and give it to him if he wasn't going to do anything more with me. He wrapped the towel around me and told me to go and get into bed. I left the bathroom, ashamed that he didn't want me after all.

The bedroom that I had prepared for my seduction suddenly seemed vulgar. I put on a nightgown that had long sleeves and buttons, an old Victorian one, not one of those I had bought for this occasion. I switched on the two lamps on the floor on either side of the bed and lit one of the joints Chris had prepared for me, hoping it would help me to overcome my humiliation. I lay there a long time, looking up at the two spots on the ceiling, trying to pretend that I didn't mind, that I hadn't wanted him anyway, but the dope only made me more aware of my body and I stubbed it out after a couple of puffs. I would have put the lights out too, if I hadn't been afraid of the dark. I put the radio on next to my bed and picked up a book and pretended to read, but none of the words made sense. Then I must have fallen asleep, because the next thing I was aware of was Tim in the bed beside me, reaching out for me, fumbling with buttons that were designed to keep Victorian gentlemen away. It took about five minutes for Tim to get that nightdress off. I didn't lift a finger to help. If he had now decided that he did want me, he'd have to bloody well work for it. And then it was off. And if my mother was watching I hoped the spotlights would blind her. As Tim's fingers moved more firmly over me, my body began to shudder and soften with delight. I leaned over and switched the radio on loudly. If Eva was watching, by God she wasn't going to listen as well.

That night I became addicted to sex with Tim. Quite soon after that I managed without the light on. I found that if I kept my eyes tightly closed it was possible not to see the other darkness. And my mother, resenting pleasure in death as she had in life, never appeared in my bedroom again.

I glowed, became almost confident. Tim was proud of both me and himself, as any good trainer has a right to be, and he loved trying to make me blush in public. 'Can't get enough of it, can you, girl?' he said in the bank, speeding the transaction considerably.

On the Sunday before he had to go back he drove me to his parents for lunch. He kept touching me up during the last three miles so that we arrived smelling of sex. His father said, 'That's a very familiar perfume you're wearing, my dear,' and his mother said, 'The thing about expensive perfume is that it's always familiar. That's why one pays through the nose for it.'

Eight

I rang Chris only once whilst Tim was home and she told me off, quite sharply for her. 'Look,' she said, 'I thought we agreed on two separate lives. One with him and one with me. So get off the phone quickly. But just tell me one thing before I hang up. Was it good?' 'Wonderful.' 'You're a lucky girl then. 'Bye.'

We didn't spend all our time in bed. It just seemed that way. On the morning of the day that he was going back to Scotland he said, 'Look, I know this is crazy and it doesn't make sense but I've really fallen in love with you.'

He looked at me expectantly so I kissed him. 'Tell you what. When you come back next time why don't you move in with me? You might as well.'

'I thought you'd never ask,' he said, swinging me round all the way down to the bedroom.

'You'll miss your train,' I said.

'There'll be others.'

Afterwards, when we were smoking the cigarettes that taste like no other in the world, the taste of nicotine filtering through saliva and sweat and come, he said, 'Next time I'm back, why don't we sell the car and get a Mini? I'm sure we wouldn't get so many fines and it would be so much easier to park.' 'Good idea,' I said drowsily. He got up and dressed and kissed me again and then I must have fallen asleep, for later there was the sensation of waking up. Alone.

It was still too early to ring Chris, so I pottered around the flat, tidying it up, but not too much. I didn't want to remove too many traces of Tim's existence in case the huge happiness I felt started to evaporate.

I was a bit behind with my proof reading so I spent the rest of the morning and the early afternoon catching up on that and then dropped the books into the publisher on my way to see Chris.

Chris was loving and welcoming and curious. She got out the ever ready gin bottle and we talked far into the night. 'I won't have to shoo you away early tonight. I have always believed that whatever your job it is extremely important to have one day off a week. In my case it seemed a good idea to make it Sunday. Most of the clergy are working, and the others are at home playing charades or whatever the hell they call their evenings *en famille*. It gives me a rest, too. A chance to catch up on my washing and bits and pieces. And it is nice to be able to read the Sunday papers actually on Sunday. It just isn't the same reading them on Monday or Tuesday.' She went and made some sandwiches and brought them back into the room. 'In fact, even for you, my darling girl, I'm not going to miss out on them. So let's just put our feet up and share them.'

That evening we ate and drank and read in the kind of comfortable silence I had only ever shared with Tim. It was early September by now, the nights were getting colder, and when we had finished and it was time for bed, Chris said, 'Why don't you sleep here tonight? That settee you're lolling on converts into a bed and I've got a sleeping bag in the cupboard. It'll be lonely going back to the flat without Tim, so you might as well make the most of my offer. It's not one I'll often make, I warn you.'

61

I smiled back at her. It did seem a good idea.

And so the months passed. When Tim was home, I spent all my time with him, and when he was away I had my books and I had Chris. I was so absurdly happy that I started keeping a diary again. I didn't want to forget this happiness.

The day before Christmas Eve, while I was waiting for Tim to collect me to go to his parents, it occurred to me that I hadn't had a period recently. I was going to my diary to check when I remembered the last one, which had been particularly bad. I had had a dreadful stomach ache, as I seemed to have had every second period since my sexual activity had started, and Tim had volunteered to go out for the Feminax and Tampax, which had made me love him more, which had made the cramps worse. I had been aware of some bangs outside and then the front door banged as well and Tim came in with a rare look of outrage on his face.

'Right,' he said, 'I'd like you to have fewer periods. In fact I'd like you to go on strike. I had no idea all this luxury was so freely available to you ladies. Sorry. Not freely. Makes me wish I were a politician. Fucking VAT on Tampax. Had a row with the bloke. He said it was because they were non-essential goods. Many women of his mother's generation had used old sheets, he said, and no wonder the country was going to the dogs, all these women expecting sanitary protection both internal and external to arrive ready-made. And there were none of your biological detergents then, either. He actually said "sanitary protection both internal and external". And he made it sound salacious. He doesn't know why women don't go out and buy ready-made babies all wrapped up in a box and if this government had any sense they'd slap VAT on abortions as well. It was incredible . . . I've never heard anyone being so offensive, and in a place you can't

62

ask him to leave. I wanted to chuck them at him and all his fascist drugs . . . '

'Hang on a minute. How can drugs be fascist?'

'They can frighten the shit out of you for a start. Jesus Christ, I simply can't believe it. That bloke shouldn't be allowed near a sponge if he was drowning. He's pornography personified. I've a good mind to go back and make a citizen's arrest.'

'Tim, my lovely, excuse me, but did you get them?'

'Yeah. Got a mortgage. Bastard. And he had the last word.'

'Tim . . . '

'Sorry, kid. Really gets up my nose. Here, take them.'

I went to the loo and called through the half-open door, 'What do you mean, he had the last word?'

'Well, I was so angry I couldn't think what to do. This great face. Film of sweat on it. So I asked for a receipt. He loved that. Made out his pen didn't work. All the old tricks. Bastard.'

I took the old one out, inserted the new, resenting the fact that there was a foreign body where Tim belonged. The chain wouldn't pull.

'But did you get it?'

'Yes, I got it. Here, look. He's written on it "internal sanitary protection for women". Asked my name. Wrote Mister at the top. Here you are, Sir. I think a lot of people will be interested to know if you can claim for this. Millions of men must feel as you do, and quite right. Why should we have to subsidise all these bitches on heat? Should come out of family allowance. Paying for pleasure is one thing, but you're paying for the withdrawal of pleasure.'

I got back into bed.

'You're making this up. We don't have mad chemists in England. Give us a hug, warm me up.'

63

'Must have a piss first, hang on.'

I pulled my knees up to try and ease the cramps. Tim came back into the room and he was trying to look stern. 'Right. No more of that. From now on, you don't put them down the loo. A little recycling is called for, I think.'

'You're all right. Only women bleed.'

'I expect they're working on it. Bent chemists. Once they get men bleeding too they can pay off the National Debt.'

He lay along the bed behind me, making it a warmer place.

And then the window opposite was suddenly filled with rockets and shooting stars. 'November 5th. I'd forgotten.'

And now, in the distance, I could hear Christmas carols. Nearly seven weeks. The front door banged and Tim arrived. He didn't say anything about being late. I did. There was a bell ringers' rehearsal at the church round the corner. It began at the exact moment when I said, 'I'm going to have a baby.' The bells pealed forth with music to be born to, and I had to say it again, too loudly.

'I'm going to have a baby.'

'You're going to have a baby?'

Tim looked at me as though he didn't understand the meaning of the words, as though the problem was nothing to do with him, as though he had no penis. I was looking in a mirror that lied. Two people looked in; two different people looked back. Didn't look back.

This stranger had exactly the same eyes as Tim. It was very shocking, that visual plagiarism.

A beat. Two. Three. Eyes locked. Deadlocked. I broke first, felt if I didn't look away my eyes would develop cataracts to protect me from his. I spoke again. Perhaps if he heard a voice he would remember how to use his own.

'Why am I so afraid?' Another beat. Four. Five. Then, his voice.

'You are not going to have this baby. I will marry you, but no baby now. O.K.? Deal?'

I half expected him to push a contract towards me. But my silence is not my signature.

It was the first row we had ever had, that day before Christmas Eve when Tim first started to barter our baby for a wedding ring. Hard to call it a row actually, since so little was said.

We drove to Tim's parents as planned, knowing that the mutual protection racket would start functioning as soon as we arrived. It was getting there that was the problem, driving through our own silences.

As we stopped outside the house, Tim reached out a cold hand and touched my fingers. No pressure, just contact.

I had not yet exchanged my vanity for gratitude and the gesture was not enough. And then the porch light came on and I saw a tear in Tim's eye and I was nearly content.

Tim's father looked like a male nurse, but was actually a doctor. His mother, a nurse, looked like a doctor from a country where the training didn't take very long. And they adored me, but if Tim had fallen in love with Myra Hindley they'd have said Wasn't she good with children?

I called them Mum and Dad. I'd never called anyone that before and at first it had seemed strange, not from a sense of betrayal or treachery as much as from a sense of being too old to begin at the beginning.

The trouble with Christmas was carols, and to Mum and Dad carols meant singing. Not singing to be confused with listening and mouthing, but real singing.

Solos and descants and no accompaniment except embarrassment.

The trouble with being pregnant at Christmas and unwillingly preparing for an abortion was also carols. And the trouble with carols is all those bleeding babies in every verse. Composing an anti-carol in the bath as hot as the gin was cold, I got as far as magenta placenta to four different tunes. It wasn't far enough, not like Bethlehem, and as I climbed out of the bath an excess of steam and too many sloes conspired to take me out of myself, and I fainted. When I came round I was lying on the bathroom floor. The door was open and I could see Tim and Dad framed in the lintel, shadowy through the evaporating steam. Mum was on her knees beside me, frowning her glasses back on to her nose. I hoped that I was the only person who noticed that her watch had stopped and that she was taking my pulse with her thumb. The towel wasn't covering me properly and as I looked down I saw that one breast was showing. I pulled the towel further up, my arm heavy and clumsy so that it brushed quite hard against my breasts and I nearly cried out with pain and surprise. Tim's face replaced his mother's now that I was decent, and as he said, 'O.K., kiddo?' it was almost as though he had never known my body. I looked at him and his eyes were what mattered, as the forgotten gentleness returned to its accustomed place.

'Let the train take the strain,' he whispered, kissing me so that I couldn't stop smiling.

'Mum, Dad, not very formal, but we're getting married.'

His father, a pub man, said Cheers. His wife must have been looking at my face upside down and imagined my smile to be the frown of a sad clown, for she stayed silent. When I had come round properly and was dressed and drinking champagne downstairs with all the others,

Dad made a clumsy toast to the happy couple and then announced that he would also like to drink a modest toast to himself and his good wife. He had been offered a very good share in a group practice in Florida and now of course they would definitely be able to go. As a matter of fact they were off in March. So there was another toast then to everyone's brilliant timing.

As Christmas passed into January, month of resolutions, I packed my case. I was really only able to talk to Tim now during surgery hours since at all other times one or other parent would pop in with an 'All right, children? No hanky panky, mind. Save it.' Because as soon as Tim had told them that marriage was the next step, I had been moved to a room of my own with Habitat catalogues and copies of *Good Housekeeping* on the bedside table. We told Mum and Dad that I had to get back to work and that seemed quite reasonable to them. It would also give them more time with Tim before they left for the States.

What I said to Tim was, 'Look, I'm going to get this over and done with, and on my own. It's the end of one thing, the beginning of another. We don't both have to start Phase Two with memories of Phase One. I must sort myself out and I'll do it more quickly if I'm on my own. Chris will look after me, she'll know what to do. You'll only be in the way, and I'd rather you met her when it's all over and forgotten, not while we're in this mess.' What I wanted to say to Tim was, 'Oh God, stop me. Tell me you've changed your mind, that you love both of us.' And when he didn't say any of those things, what I wanted to go on to say was, 'Is being pregnant a reward or a punishment, and if so, for what? And is abortion still illegal if you don't want it done, if it wasn't your idea, if you are innocent? Can you say I did it because I love you? Does that give me a free pardon by proxy or will they order a retrial? Why won't you ask me why I don't ask you why I have to have this done? One more thing. Perhaps until now, I have never been afraid: that must be why I have never needed courage before now. Will we be all right, Tim? Tim? Can you hear me?'

Obviously not, since he drove me to the station without crashing. He was clearly not distracted. His hands on the wheel were steady, no white knuckles on that side of the car, no grinding of gears, no swearing.

But when he turned round from getting my ticket his voice was unsteady. 'Sadie, I will never ever buy you a single ticket to anywhere again. After this I will always be with you; and if I'm not then you will have a return.'

'Cheap day,' I said, to conjure up as my last memory his face smiling. I think that was the first time I realised how easy it was to make a man laugh, even against his will.

Just outside London all the lights in my compartment went out. The moment of terror as I searched for the communication cord was followed by relief when the lights came back on and gratitude that I had not after all had arms long enough to reach the cord. Then came anger. Suppose I had been beaten, raped, interfered with, robbed, molested or approached by a man with a curette in his hand, what then? A child, a not very tall old lady, a small young lady or one doubled over in pain? How would they reach that safety chain, or were we fair game, minority groups not yet registered in the game of statistics? I had once been made to stand in the corridor as a child for putting my feet on a seat.

I got a pen out of my bag and wrote on the wall Sad Sad Sadie was here, but it wouldn't penetrate the layer of grease, so I wrote it on the wooden window surround, Sad Sad Sadie is here, in the present tense.

Nine

Chris was in bed when I arrived. I hadn't rung her, but my 'I'm pregnant' on the doorstep was enough. She called over her shoulder into the bedroom, 'Come on. Out. It's people like you who get these poor girls into trouble in the first place. I'm sorry, you'll have to go. Business and pleasure are incompatible. I've always said that, now I see that I mean it. I'll ring you when things are better, convenient. O.K.?'

I was miming and muttering on the pavement, 'Oh God, I'll go away, come back later, I never thought you'd be . . . Oh God . . . ' and then I was cut short by the sight of an elderly Asian humming 'Oh God, our help in ages past', shuffling out into the hall, fumbling with his fly buttons. He interrupted his song to smile at me and say, with a little bow, 'You and I must both thank God that I am an English count and you are an English cunt. I needed one more minute. So you know for next time.'

And then he was the wrong side of the door and I was safely inside. 'Oh Chris, I am so sorry . . . '

'Shut up about being sorry. It takes three cans of hairspray just to get him the size of my little finger. One more minute, bollocks. He's been here four hours already. But they're very good to me at his embassy and they always apologise for sending him, and pay me double. In advance.'

'But who is he?'

'Not my friendly neighbourhood rent boy, that's for sure. But mock me not . . . nor him. He could be useful. He's a diplomat.'

'Not your problem, then.'

'I can't share everything. How many weeks?'

'Nine. Ish. I can't have it.'

'Early bird catchee baby best. We'll talk later. Unpack. I'll make some calls.'

Chris made a lot of calls, some appointments and not enough coffee. 'It's a damn' nuisance my doctor's just gone away for three months. I call him Doctor Zhivago, can't pronounce his real name, he came over from Hungary in '56. I've never charged him a penny and he'd do anything for me. Or you, now that he knows about you. Anyway, let's try for a legal abortion first. Go and see these people tomorrow. Here's a Mogadon. You need a good sleep.'

I saw four separate people in the following weeks, but it was no good. None of them seemed able to tell the difference between bad and sad and mad. It was mostly my own fault, because I wouldn't let them inside my head. They said I was perfectly sane and healthy and refused to sign the important form. I was so stupidly innocent then. Now I would talk them into believing whatever I wanted them to believe, and make them think it was all their own idea.

Chris brought a tray in to me every morning now; apparently I was having nightmares so she came in chatting brightly.

On February 2nd, Candlemas, she put the tray beside the bed as usual. Also as usual she put the radio on and banged around to wake me out of my fragile misery.

'Right. We've tried doing it legally. Now for other means. There is this woman I know who lives near

70

Purley, but she travels. That's how she got into this racket in the first place actually. Kept driving pregnant friends over potholes. And those were people who wanted their babies. Anyway, she got such a name for herself, and she's averagely greedy but at least she'll do it without asking you if you ever wanted to fuck your mother's dog. She's not cheap, but I've rung her and she's coming up tonight.'

'But I haven't got any money left. Not enough anyway.'

'Worry not. The only thing marriage taught me was to always keep enough money in the house for an abortion. Even now I still keep it. Just because I'm too old doesn't mean I can't spend it. It's there for all of us. In trust.'

I was silent. If I'd been a spontaneous toucher I would have hugged Chris, but I hugged myself instead, feeling pregnant for the first time. Today I felt that my body actually contained a jelly baby. And could contain it.

I ate some of the breakfast that Chris had provided. It made her feel as though she was doing something helpful.

The rest of the day I spent curled up in the same position as my baby, rather like my mother's Madonna and Child, except that the baby was inside me and not in my arms where I really wanted it to be.

I took three Mogadon and slept away the hours until the Purley Maid was due to arrive to take away from me the only thing in the world that was mine, that I wanted.

I suppose the sound of the door opening woke me and I saw Chris and my baby's bailiff standing looking at me. She looked like a Young Conservative doing a sociology degree at the Open University. I looked at Chris. She nodded her head without actually moving it. The woman put her bag on the floor as she spoke. 'Right,' said a voice to forget, 'these are the terms. I'm doing you a favour.

Anything that happens after I leave this house, any problems, are yours. Nothing to do with me. O.K.? Go to the lavatory and we'll begin. But first I'll have the money, because I don't have much time. It'll hurt a bit but don't make a fuss, it'll only make it last longer. And I assume you've got cash. I don't do this for love, you know.'

Sitting on the lavatory, stroking my small bellyful of baby for the last time, I wondered what my mother would have said if confronted with that truth? Argued probably, rather than sacrifice Purgatory. Do it for love. Don't do it for love. Not much difference, really.

That is almost all I remember, 'I don't do this for love.' It was so much the opposite of my mother's cry that it was possible to imagine both attitudes as right. Certainly I was wrong. I know that because a staff nurse kept telling me so when I came round in the hospital. Being in the wrong was the only familiar thing in the midst of all that pain and starch and censure as I was prepared for theatre.

The anaesthetic made me sleep throughout the night and I was woken up the following morning by the ward sister, who had not been on duty when I was admitted. She pushed my hair back off my face and smiled at me, using her eyes as well as her mouth. 'Telegram,' she said. 'A telegram for me?' I said. 'But only one person knows I'm here.' She smiled again. 'It's not only God that moves in mysterious ways; sometimes the Post Office does too. How's the pain?'

'I can't imagine or remember its absence.'

'I have an injection for you right here.' She must have been wonderful at darts because it didn't hurt at all. As she rubbed my thigh and pulled the sheets back over me, she pulled a chair over and said, 'Let's have a little chat while the pethidine has time to work, to take your mind off the pain in your body if not your head.'

'I wish you'd been here when I was admitted,' I said. She nodded her head and I could see that I mattered, and as a way of thanking her I said, 'I got told off.'

'Yes, I'm sure you did. Technically she's one of the best staff nurses I've ever had, but she thinks moral judgments are as important as I think they're none of our business. I dread days off in case girls like you come in, because I know that she will have made the whole nightmare experience into a daymare as well. She's not even a Catholic. But now I'm making moral judgments too. Everyone copes in different ways.'

'How do you cope?'

'Anger. Not for you girls, though. Half of it is aimed at the back-street abortionists, particularly when they're women doing what they do to other women. It's a good job you don't know her full name, your Purley Queen. Utah's paste, indeed. The other half is directed towards that lot in Parliament who make the abortion laws. They should come here and do my job. Or change sex, make a mistake, a human mistake. They make enough in their White Papers, don't even pretend they're typing errors. Imagine if they had periods. We'd have monthly Hiroshimas. We'd be on World War Six Hundred by now. My God, if men ovulated you could get abortions at the bus stop.'

I was starting to feel drowsy and what she was saying reminded me of Tim. She stood up. 'I can see that you're getting blurry round the edges. Try and doze. Oh, and perhaps I should pretend to be a politician and deny that I ever said anything about moral judgments. Silly thing is that I like most of the men I know. But then they don't think they know what's best for me better than I do. See you later.'

Just as I was dropping off I remembered the telegram.

73

I opened it. 'DON'T DO IT   THREE-WAY WEDDINGS CHEAPER   NO BRIDESMAIDS NEEDED   RING ME   LOVE YOU TIM.'

Even then I couldn't cry. Tears filled my eyes, but finding no escape, barbed-wired their way down into my empty belly.

Ten

When they said I could go home I asked Chris if I could go there, to her flat. She had been to see me in hospital most days and I had discovered that Tim had found her phone number quite by chance on the scrap of paper where my mother had written it those few short months ago. She wouldn't tell him where I was or what had happened but had finally agreed to send me the telegram he dictated to her over the phone. Her loyalty to me was still a rare and special thing, for he could be very persuasive and now he was frantic with worry. But because I had told her I wanted no contact with him until it was over she had remained adamant. Then Chris told me he had had to go abroad again.

I think I felt that by going back to Chris, to the source of such physical and emotional disorientation, I would somehow be able to annihilate the pain. And if I couldn't, then Tim would still be there. He had to be kept separate from that pain, protected from the idea that it was in any way related to him, in case he offered to bear it for me himself, not knowing that he would be unable to.

Chris had begun her life with me as a name and a telephone number in a dead woman's envelope. And then in a way she had become the reincarnation of that dead woman, an astonishing transfiguration into all the things I had craved from Eva so hopelessly for so long. We had spoken about her briefly on that first meeting and since then I had almost forgotten that there was a link between them. Chris was Chris. Tim was Tim. Eva was dead and it was as though she had never existed, as though my lie about her to Tim had become the truth. I had been sent home from the hospital because they needed the bed, not because the agony of the salpingitis the Purley Maid had exchanged for my baby had diminished. I was still on antibiotics and strong analgesics. Bedrest was the only other treatment I needed, and this, and more, Chris willingly provided.

But something important had changed and it was as though I had just discovered the existence and meaning of the word curiosity, for now Chris too had been involved in causing me pain.

On the afternoon of the second day, when the level of discomfort was high enough for the source to be irrelevant, I looked at Chris as she came in with a tea tray. I had not known that I was going to speak; I simply found myself talking.

'Tell me about Eva, Chris. Enough to help me understand my past lack of curiosity. I don't want to know but it matters now, it seems important today. First lover. First abortion. First emptiness. First strength. You caused me physical pain and it was like a gift. Her mental pain was hardly noticeable. But why didn't she care? Who was she? How did you know her?'

'Your tea's getting cold.' Chris sat silently for a few seconds. Then she looked at me and said quickly, 'She did care once, before she wanted to. And after that she forgot. They said she only recognised herself in a two-way mirror. She should have been ugly and she believed them. In the end I think she thought if her behaviour was ugly she would stop being beautiful. She wanted to be me. Sometimes she was, with no mirrors or lights. We'd dress up as each other. I'd wear her beautiful clothes, she'd wear mine – I was never smart, always scruffy. Didn't seem much point in making an effort. I was ugly and that was that, it didn't even bother me. Her all scruffy, dim lights, feeling ugly, that made her happy, real, herself, not all those expectations people always had of her. She loved your father. He was my husband. I tried to give him to her. Funny thing was he only wanted me – we were shabby but we laughed. He came in once when we were being each other, quite early one November evening, no lights on, me in her pretty clothes, she in my old things. He was drunk and made love to her thinking it was me. It was the only thing I ever gave her that mattered, that night. Next summer, of course, you were born; and then one night she saw us making love, heard me cry out as she had done that once. She couldn't punish him or me because she loved us. Punished everyone else instead, perhaps. She didn't know you, decided she never would, so she could punish herself. She tried to give you to us. But he wouldn't have it, your father. Mind you, he didn't know that, he didn't want anyone else but me. And of course he never knew he'd made love to her. Two brief disastrous marriages. Then Jock – all that travelling all those years. We didn't know you'd been sent away, weren't with them, we'd lost touch by then. Well, we didn't exactly lose it: Jock threw it away.'

Chris said all that as though she was reading aloud from a faded manuscript, auditioning for a part she did not want. So when she asked me, as she was pouring more tea, 'Is that enough? Do you need to know anything else now?' I wanted to say No, that's fine, now I understand it all. I looked at Chris, planning to say exactly that, wishing I had never asked, but the words wouldn't come out. Chris looked ten years older but even that evidence of her misery couldn't silence me yet.

'It's more than enough in many ways because it tells me so little and that's good and it tells me so much and that's bad and it doesn't explain anything that makes sense and that is as it should be, it's too late to make sense of the past now that I'm embarking on my future. But there is one thing. One question. Then no more. Please?'

Chris shrugged, imagining that the damage was done, that I would go and Eva would haunt her again.

'How did you meet each other?'

'Nobody could ever work that out, our closeness. Eva, delicate, refined, fastidious, beautiful, intelligent, born to be pampered and desired. Me, tough, coarse, stupid, ugly, common, born to be rejected. The only advantage I had over her, although she never knew it, and would not have understood it, was that I loved fucking. As you know, I still do, even though I should know better at my age. It means I do it in the dark mostly now, which is a shame. I used to love sunbeams on bodies; like spotlights from Heaven. And of course I have to be paid sometimes. I save all that though. There's nothing immoral about it. Soon I'll have to start paying for it myself, but I won't go short. She seemed to have everything, Eva. Yet knowing what I had, I felt so sorry for her, because actually she had nothing.'

Chris smiled, eyes reflecting remembered pleasure so innocently that her ugliness became beauty.

I was intrigued and impressed and did not interrupt. Chris then pretended to be shocked by what she had said, rolled her eyes and made a mock Sign of the Cross. She got up to draw the curtains, and so when she spoke again her back was turned.

'I'm sorry, I still haven't answered your question. Got a bit carried away. You asked me how we'd met didn't you?'

78

'Yes, but it doesn't matter. It doesn't seem important now.'

Chris turned back towards the fire and she looked more her old self, middle-aged, grey hair all over the place, lumpy confused body, slightly arthritic fingers, wrinkled lisle stockings.

She fished in her pocket for her cigarettes and matches. Player's No. 6 in a crumpled packet. 'I can't always get Woodbines now, isn't it silly? These are tipped. Would you like one?'

It seemed important to say yes, so I took one. The matches were all dead and so she had to light her cigarette from the gas fire, poking it through the bars, nearly setting her hair on fire. I lit mine from hers, but then she went back in front of the fire and knelt down facing me.

'You're wrong, it does matter, it is important. I've never told anyone before. But then nobody asked, and it was so long ago. Perhaps you'll wish you hadn't asked me how we met. But we didn't have any choice. Eva is — was — my sister.'

There was a silence so brief that it seemed eternal and it was the first time for days that my body was totally failing to register any kind of pain at all. I, who had been unable to move for days, actually leapt out of bed with a shout and fell on my knees in front of Chris and flung my arms around her, hugging her as I had never hugged anyone, not even Tim.

'I can't believe it. I'm not alone, is that what you're saying? I can't believe it,' and I was crying or laughing, or she was, because our faces were wet.

She held my face in her two hands. 'I can't believe it either. I thought you'd be ashamed, I was too frightened to tell you.'

'Ashamed? Because I'm not alone? You're mine. You're mine. You're really mine.'

Eleven

My abdominal pain maintained its miraculous recession, and five days later I could hardly feel it. Tim had returned the day before and had rung, but I had not spoken to him, knowing that hearing his voice would return me to the present, wanting just a little longer with Chris.

Finally she confronted me. 'Sadie, you know I love you dearly, but it's time for you to go home. You're better now, I can see it in your face, you look really good. You belong with Tim now. Besides, I'm not going to vanish; I've been here twenty years and I'm not a sitting tenant for nothing. Anyway, I have my clients to consider.'

She passed me the telephone, but I did not pick it up. She sighed, a mixture of resignation and feigned reluctance. 'We've talked non-stop for days now. I'm beginning to get a sore throat. You know me in a way no one but your father did. Better, actually. He died thinking it was sex with him I loved so much. I don't know what he must have thought after that. Do you ever think stars are really peepholes so they can check up on us, make sure we're behaving ourselves? I think that's why God invented roofs. I'll see you again very soon. It doesn't need Solomon to sort you out. You don't want to leave me because I've given you a past, but Tim is giving you a future and they tend to last longer. I'm happy to share you with him; I like what you've told me about him. Thank God he thinks sex is for human beings not frogs. Oh, to be young now . . . you've no idea what a sense of wasted time most of us tadpoles have. It's all ahead of you, the things that are behind me. Don't feel guilt or jealousy or have inhibitions and don't feel it is your duty only to give. Taking can be more important sometimes. And when desire goes, don't stick around. There's the phone. Ring Tim. Be nice. See what happens. As long as the fucking is good, stay; when it's not, go. Don't hang around hopefully, because desire, once it's gone, doesn't ever come back. I was lucky. Your father died young, before we had time to become a habit. Ring him. You have no more excuses. You look well, your pain has gone, he loves you. Don't throw that away or you'll end up having to get it on H.P., like me.'

When I heard Tim's voice I felt the stirring of another kind of abdominal discomfort. I spoke fast. 'Hello. Everything's fine. I'm fit for human consumption again. See you in an hour. Listen out for me, I haven't got my keys. 'Bye.'

It would be very, very good to see him again. While I was packing Chris made me a cup of tea. My small, optimistically small, case did not take long to fill, and when I had finished Chris clinked teacups with me and said, 'Cheers, my darling. Twenty minutes, the cab.'

'Cheers. Can I see those photographs again? Just in case I need reminding, tomorrow, that it is really all true?'

They were so old they were nearly sepia, but Eva and Chris were reproduced eleven times, from babies to toddlers to adolescents. In all of them Eva had her arms round Chris, protecting her from a world that would hold more terrors for the protector. Even then the photographer lied; Eva looked confident and happy, Chris insecure and withdrawn.

I put the pictures down, saying, 'That the camera cannot lie is a lie. It cannot tell the truth.'

Chris qualified my opinion. 'Sometimes it can. I've seen a very truthful cow. And ordinary people can look right. Beauty and ugliness are the problems. Beauty must be seen to be superior, ugliness must look grateful for the lens attention.' She put them away.

'Don't forget that Tim must never know. Maybe in a few years time I can be a long lost aunty from Australia, but telling him now would mean telling him you lied about Eva. You love him, I see it in your face. And he loves you. But if you tell him you lied his love will evaporate. It is the one sure and certain way to kill what there is between you. Not yet, perhaps, not while he still wants you, but it would happen. If you tell him, you may as well not get in that cab. The first lie is the equivalent of the last if he finds out, because love is ninety per cent trust. Without it you only have desire and, alone, even that becomes infected before it runs its average course of three years. Honesty is the only currency of love that no one can ever devalue.'

There was a silence. The minicab hooted. The silence continued.

Then, 'Off you go, then. Ring me any time.'

We walked to the door.

'Sadie, believe everything I've said. I may be an old whore, but I'm an honest one.'

'I wish you were my mother.'

'I wish I could say I was. But that would be a lie.'

We both smiled, but it hurt.

'I love you, Chris. So much wasted time. Talk to you soon.'

'I love you too.'

Down the steps to the cab. A pause.

'Sadie, it goes both ways, lying. He will do it to you, and you won't want to know. You'll think your love is different, stronger.'

'It is.'

'No. It doesn't exist, that kind of love. You must believe me. However small the lie, as soon as you recognise it, leave.'

'No second chance?'

'No second chance. It may take time but all you will be left with is suspicion. Don't waste years trying to prove me wrong. Start by asking him why he made you have an abortion. You'll know if he's telling the truth. Love you. Take care. But ask him. 'Bye.'

I sat in the cab, afraid, rehearsing silently all the way home, 'Why did you make me have an abortion?'

'Why did you make me have an abortion?' I said, hearing the minicab drive away. The arms that had been outstretched to welcome me fell empty to his sides.

'Do you want the truth?'

'That's all I do want.'

We stood in the hallway, looking at each other.

'I thought I had the clap when you got pregnant.'

'Do you want applause?' I said with a voice that cracked like a nutshell.

'No. I fucked someone at a party. I don't know who, just a drunken woman smelling of sex. She followed me into the lavatory and locked the door. She looked at me and she said, "Hello, I love you." She'd been doing it most of the evening to any man she saw alone. But I only heard the words. I was so grateful I put the light out. I was drunk too and I tried to pretend she was you, you saying what you'd never said. She was so drunk she hardly noticed. Neither did I, except that it wasn't you.'

'Mick's party?'

'Yes.'

'But you came home and made love to me. We went on all night.'

'Yes. In silence. I imagined you saying what she had said. You didn't of course. You never have.'

'Perhaps I'm dyslexic.'

'Then I got that discharge after a few weeks. I went to the clinic in Scotland. And when I came home you said you were pregnant. I thought our baby would be born mad or blind . . .'

'But we made love at Christmas . . .'

'I know. Because I'd had treatment. They don't take any risks on those rigs. They have to send the samples off to the mainland, so if it looks suspicious they treat you anyway. By the time I went back up there and got the negative result it was too late, you'd gone to Chris and I had to wait until I was back here to try and find out where you were, try and find a phone number for her.'

'Why didn't you tell me?'

'You once said you were afraid of the truth.'

'Yes. And now I'm afraid of lies.' And I knew that Tim had told me the truth although it hurt more than a lie would have done.

Twelve

Three weeks later Tim and I were married. Seeing each other again after those miserable weeks of separation was wonderful: I fell in love with him all over again – more intensely than ever. Whether this was because I now had some identity of my own or because he had told me the truth when I had been prepared for a lie I don't know. I had told him almost nothing about the abortion when he had asked me, finding that I really did want to protect him from the sheer awfulness of it, not wanting to burden him with guilt and perhaps hoping that by remaining silent it would go away. I think in fact that if I had wanted to tell him I would have found it quite difficult; the conversations with Chris seemed to have almost totally eclipsed it.

Our wedding was as religious as I could have wished. I had never been to one before and was afraid that register offices might leave the job unfinished, that it was possible to get into the wrong queue and discover too late that one was a widow or a mother instead of a bride. I had imagined torn lino and the smell of Dettol and district surveyors and no feeling of permanence. Instead I was moved nearly to tears by the flowers and sincerity and honesty, so that as well as the spoken vows I also made a private vow not to let this kind registrar down either. If we had been married in the Vatican by the Pope it could not have been more binding, moving, serious or committed. No unction could be more supreme than this sacrament. I felt my nuns would be proud of me and not ashamed, as I had privately feared. I even thought they would not object to the No Confetti signs that Tim's parents, our sole witnesses, did not notice until too late. It was the only sour note, that hint of Satanic overtime. That and Chris's absence at the ceremony. I had begged her to be there but she had absolutely refused, saying that she would find it so emotional that Tim would be sure to wonder afterwards why a comparative stranger was weeping as though losing a daughter.

However, as we came out into the sharp March sunshine, rather slowly because Tim's mother was trying to urge the forbidden confetti out into the street with her hat, someone else stepped forward and tipped another packet of confetti all over us. It seemed legal on a public thoroughfare, or at any rate there was no sign saying that it was forbidden. I turned round and came face to face with Chris. She gave me a quick frown and then grinned inanely at the pair of us in an I-am-a-total-stranger way. When she spoke it was directly to Tim. 'Oh, don't mind me, love. I come up here every week to throw confetti at the weddings, because I know it's not allowed inside and that's not a proper way to start married life, no little bits of paper in your hair. Good luck to both of you, you're a beautiful couple,' and then she disappeared into the crowd that had collected.

Tim's dad said, 'Who was that funny old girl?' but neither his question nor his wife's 'It doesn't matter, gypsies are always lucky. Remember that one when we were married, outside the church?' could take away the fact that Chris had been there.

As they hailed a taxi to take us off for lunch at the Connaught, Tim put his arms round me.

'You're really mine now,' he said, as though he couldn't quite believe his luck, as though it was very important. If I had committed some unspeakable crime and my punishment was to have one of my certainties smashed beyond recognition, I would rather die than admit my surest certainty and the most vulnerable was that Tim really loved me. Even then when I was so sure. Maybe he loved me more than I loved him, impossible though that seems. If I had only been able to say so, or at least had understood that Tim, too, needed to hear the words spoken, that showing it was no substitute for saying it.

He hugged me again and repeated what he had just said. 'You're mine, you're really mine. Let's make it a quick lunch. We have some unfinished business, remember? We have to go home and make a baby.'

But we didn't. Make a baby I mean. The months passed, but so did the blood. We weren't worried at first. There was all the performance of getting Tim's parents off to America for a start, and all the Last Suppers that entailed. As it happened, their flight was in the morning so we had a Last Breakfast as well. Then Tim had to go out to the Gulf a couple of times, so we had longer separations, but that was all right too, for it meant I had more time for Chris and my books, still loving Tim as much as ever, but knowing he would be back with me as soon as possible.

It was after we had been married for nearly a year that I started to worry a bit. Tim triggered my anxiety one night when he said, 'Your breasts are so beautiful. They are my babies,' licking and stroking, waking them up for his two o'clock feed. Suddenly self-conscious, I moved away. 'Breasts,' I said, 'would be so much nicer to look at if there were no nipples, if they were always smooth and soft. Like your skin. Why do men go on about women having soft skin? It's as phony as pregnancy making women so much more beautiful. All skin is soft.'

'This bit down here seems rather hard. I wonder if I could have a second opinion? I want you. Very much. I want you.'

I climbed on top of him, as wet inside as my mother's mouth had been once.

The next morning I told Tim that I wanted to go to a fertility clinic, or at least have some tests done. And so began the long wearying visits to the specialist clinic to which the abortion hospital referred me, when the first thing inserted into me every morning was a hard, cold thermometer instead of a hard, warm penis and lying on my back with my legs in the air being looked up by strangers didn't even make me embarrassed any more, just cold. Tim, we knew, was all right, and I was grateful that he wasn't cocky when this was officially confirmed. The sense of failure that Eva and Jock had injected into me as a child but which Tim and Chris had diluted with their transfusions of love and support began to be familiar again when I was alone. I found that I could not really talk about my intermittent despair to either of them in case I burdened them with guilt, so I suppose that on the surface things continued much as before; when Tim was home I was a wife, when he was away I was a daughter. 'There's plenty of time,' Tim and the doctors kept saying as the news continued to be bad, as though time had the remotest connection with a blocked Fallopian tube and an empty uterus.

I had hardly noticed at first that all the doctors were men. We always arranged the appointments for the times when Tim was at home, for they said that they liked to see us as a couple. They also said that we had everything going for us; we were young, we were healthy, my God, we were even married. Besides, I was brought up to believe in men. Their decisions were final. I never doubted them. Now, of course, I could recognise a liar, could create one at will, but before the anger improved my perception I agreed with all they said, wasting so much of the time they said I had in abundance.

Then Tim's mum sent me a large parcel of baby clothes with an accompanying note saying that she was sure we would be needing these soon and they had given her an itchy rash on her fingers, knitting them in all that sunshine, but some good had come out of it and if Baby got bad nappy rash not to worry, they had this marvellous cream . . .

Tim had only been gone two days but I suddenly did not want to wait for our next appointment, I needed to see someone now. So I rang and when they asked me which doctor I was with I played dumb and pretended I had forgotten the name but it was a woman and if they said the name I would remember it. Easy, they said, we've only got one woman here, Dr Connors. 'That's it,' I replied, and could I see her urgently as something had changed slightly and I had been told to report any change. The girl on the phone, terrified that I might go into details, gave me an appointment for the following day. Just me, no Tim.

Dr Connors must have been older than me, but she looked younger. She smiled and I realised how alone I had felt until now. She examined me, read my notes, frowned, checked back and frowned again. As I sat opposite her, fully clothed now, she offered me a cigarette. As I inhaled she left the room with a back-in-a-minute gesture that I couldn't interpret.

She came back with two cups of coffee and I smiled in

surprised delight as she sat down and I began to lift my cup. She fiddled with the handle of hers as she said, 'May I call you Sadie?'

I nodded my head, swallowing, realising too late that the coffee had sugar in it. 'It's my name.'

'Sadie, there's been a slight, well, something I don't like has happened. I'm sticking my neck out by telling you, but I don't see that I have any choice. I work here because I like women, care about them, and part of that caring is a dislike of dishonesty.'

I put my coffee down and then abruptly picked it up and drank it all down in one, sugar and all.

I looked at her and nodded my head slightly. She held my eyes in a way the men never had.

The coffee had not been as warming as I would have wished it to be.

'Sadie, your husband, Tim, was told nearly a year ago, after the first series of tests, that you could never, ever, have a child. Not after that septic abortion.'

And of course, the world didn't stop. It just turned a little more slowly. I suppose that's what they meant when they said I had plenty of time.

Thirteen

I went, of course, straight to Chris. I hadn't seen her for a few weeks, as we had been on holiday and before that she had been away for a few days, but we had talked on the phone as usual. This day, I was so distraught by Tim's treachery that I didn't stop to ring and let her know that I was coming. It was a long time before she opened the door and for a moment I hoped I had come to the wrong house by mistake, for she was almost unrecognisable. I could see, confronted with it for the second time in my life, that she was going to die. As I followed her into her little sitting room I had a further shock for the room was almost completely bare of all the little bits and pieces that had been so important to her. Often when we'd been talking about things that mattered she would un- consciously touch one or other of them as if to lend credibility to remembered happiness. 'I needed the money,' she shrugged, seeing me look with horror at the room that now resembled my own flat when I had first seen it.

'Business not so good then?' I said clumsily, trying to enter her private world, hoping that she would continue to allow me access to it, expecting her special smile of acknowledged complicity.

Instead, for the first and last time I saw tears in her eyes which were not of laughter.

'Business kaput. Gone into permanent liquidation.'

I frowned, confused, uncomprehending, afraid suddenly of touching her, this special lady I had formerly embraced as freely as though we were Siamese twins. She blew her nose and I registered another unconscious shock seeing her use a roll of loo paper and not one of her pretty lace handkerchieves. It took her a long time to blow back all the tears. Then she tried to grin, failed and gave up.

'Darling Sadie. I always thought God was a practical joker. He had to be, otherwise he would have invented a more dignified way of fucking. I never thought of him as a sadist before though. Eva, who hated sex, could have gone on enjoying it with one breast, even with a bad back. Me, he's punishing for something I never thought was a sin; all the moving parts that gave me pleasure they want to take away.'

I wasn't taking anything in, didn't know what she was talking about and her eyes clouded over again as she looked at me.

'Mumbo jumbo doesn't work any more. Sadie, I love you, and loving doesn't mean lies or games, as I keep telling you, so we'll have to be honest together. I've got cancer, too, like Eva. But in my vagina, my cervix, my uterus and my ovaries. I never did do things by halves. They want to do an operation. A total pelvic clearance, I think they call it; but . . . they're not taking away the only thing that ever gave me pleasure before you came back to me. It may be diseased, but I'm keeping it. I hardly ever gave it away for nothing, and I'm not going to start now. O.K.?'

And then at last we reached out for each other. And I repeated over and over again the words that Eva had made it so difficult for me to say, 'I love you, I love you, I love you.'

I didn't tell her why I had called originally. I felt so

devastated by what she had told me that my problem became irrelevant. I rocked Chris in my arms as though she were the child I would never have, until finally we were both soothed by the motion. I stroked her hair, kissing its coarseness and whispering 'I love you' so many times that it ceased to be a foreign language, became nearly familiar.

Finally, when it was completely dark we found ourselves comforted and peaceful and even drowsy. Chris moved away and put lights on and as we blinked in the brightness the grief surrounding us lost a dimension and became manageable, as it had to if it was to be endured.

'Cup of tea or a drink?' Chris said, as though I had just arrived.

'I think a drink would be a good idea,' I said, not breaking any rules by referring to what had gone before, not implying that we needed one.

'Well, there's gin or gin,' Chris said, on her knees in front of the drinks cupboard that looked as though it were built only to contain sweet sherry. I had not drunk gin since the day I fainted at Tim's parents' house when I had been pregnant and drinking gin in an attempt not to be.

'Can I change my mind, Chris? I must be more English than I thought. A cuppa seems a better idea. No, you sit down, I'll make it.'

In the kitchen I did everything incredibly fast but as though it was in slow motion. I had tried to show Tim I loved him although I could never say it. Now I was finally able to say it and mean it to Chris but was totally unable to show it in a way that would prove how absolutely I meant it. If only I could give Chris the parts of my own body that were going to kill her it would begin to make sense. My sterility wouldn't matter because I would still be giving somebody life. My

93

conviction, that it was more important to show love than to say it, strengthened into a helpless rage at the uselessness of my own body. God had made it too easy, giving people words to substitute for deeds. If only all the world were dumb.

We drank the tea in silence, for there seemed nothing to say, not after all the times Chris — and Tim too, I had thought — had demonstrated love's definition as honesty. It made it more difficult, being unable to fall back on the panacea of platitudes and euphemisms and false optimism, but our silence was uncontaminated by guilt.

Chris put down her half-empty cup, wrinkling her nose and saying, 'I think I'll just have a little tiny gin, darling, if you don't mind. I'm sure it's better for me than tannin, and anyway, you make lousy tea. Funny thing is, so did Eva. It's about the only way you take after her, apart from your looks. Your father, now, he really knew how to make it. I used to call him Earl Grey sometimes. Introduced him as that once to a friend of your mother's, some ghastly snob. When she said goodbye, she called me Lady Grey. Those were good days, him and me. Then all those long lonely years alone. Now it's gone full circle and I've ended up being happy again, having you back. You'll never know how much you've given me. I read once, some article, that something like ninety-eight per cent of women with breast cancer have been through a very bad time and are recovering when they find the cancer. I know mine isn't breast cancer but it's nearly the same, it's still the places that make me a woman, affect my hormones. I think that's so savage. So, so savage. When things are going to be all right, *bam*. Proves one thing I'd always suspected, anyway. God's a Tory. All these cuts.'

I didn't smile, reserving the small joke to enjoy later, when I would need it.

94

'Yes, it is savage. But then perhaps it makes it easier. If everything else in your life were bad you wouldn't be able to cope with that too. I don't know . . . I don't begin to understand any of it.'

'If I were younger I'd declare war on it. But I'm so tired all I can do is wave a white flag. There's this terrible sense of outrage. All through your life you get let down, by people, places, things, Southern Region. The last thing you expect is that you'll do it to yourself, that your own body will turn traitor. Your own body: the one thing you think you have some control over. I think if I were young that outrage would give me enormous strength. You'll have to be strong for me.'

'I wish I could have it for you.'

'Don't you ever dare say that again. I've had twenty-odd years longer than you. And lots of them were good. And even during the bad ones I had a lot of laughs. That's what I'd like to pass on to you, laughter. Tears are such a waste of time.'

I, who had only recently learned to cry, nodded my head. Another silence, except for the clink of the ice in Chris's gin. That clink reminded me of the clink of money once when I had turned my purse upside down on a glass table, and the coins had made a similar sound.

'That's what I wanted to ask you, Chris. When I saw how bare everything was this afternoon you said you needed the money, but I remember once you said that if you had to go into hospital for something serious, you'd go privately. That always amazed me, it was so unlike you. But you're not going to have the operation, so why do you need money so badly?'

'I thought I'd explained why I said I'd be a private patient if I was dying. Let me tell you that first. I suppose partly it was a flippant thing to say, but I did mean it if it was for something serious. I probably won't explain this

95

very well. It's just that — well, I'm sure there are lots of people who think that I'm a bit of an old scrubber, and maybe to them I am. But I don't think that I am and I know that you don't think I am and I don't care about anyone else, not any more, because in a funny kind of way, I've always had some dignity. Not publicly, privately. And the thought of being seriously ill and in pain in a big ward where people hear you cry out when it hurts and know you smell if you've been incontinent and see before you do that you're dying makes me go cold. Losing your independence and being called lovey or poppet by a nurse, who maybe calls you that because she can't remember your name — I really couldn't bear that, that total loss of dignity. And I'm not confusing it with pride. Your father died in a big ward in a National Health hospital and I've never forgotten those few days. Everybody looking and listening, no privacy. Not just him, several others at the same time. And he wasn't even old. If you die in a public ward, it's like dying on stage, with an audience. The worst thing, the very worst, hypocritical thing, the thing I never forgot, was that I saw people dying when I was waiting for him to die, three of them during the days that I was there; there wasn't any peace about it, all bustle and fiddling about with thermometers and shouting to see if they were unconscious or asleep and people staring and saying to their visitors, "I don't think he'll last long", and noise and laughter and trolleys banging and a sense of no one caring and life going on. Until they actually died. Then, my God, what a difference. Hushed voices, curtains drawn, an extraordinary quiet. Do you know what they do once you're dead? Once a doctor has pronounced that life is over? They straighten the body, close the eyes and the mouth, cross the hands on the breast, tidy the hair. Then they draw the curtains around you for an hour. And do you know the reason they give? A mark of respect.'

She got up and poured more gin into her glass. There was no tonic. She laughed, a harsh, dry croak. It was the only time I ever heard her both angry and bitter. 'A mark of respect. Huh. The time those poor sods need dignity and respect is before they die, not afterwards. What use is it then? Don't you agree it's a little bit too late? Some of them might not even have died if they'd had a little bit of peace and quiet. They probably die to get away from the noise.'

She gulped at the gin and lit one of her No. 6 cigarettes. The nicotine acted like a tranquilliser and she turned to me with her familiar loving gentleness. 'Oh, Sadie, I'm sorry. I've wanted to say that to someone for twenty years now. Bottled it up, been angry about it. Even cried about it. But I should never have said it to you. I wanted to say it to someone who could have changed it. Not you and your innocence. I started to shout about it from the public gallery at the House of Commons once, when my M.P. didn't answer any of my letters, but they bundled me out before I'd even finished one sentence. My own fault, I suppose. It never works when you try to let someone know how much you've been hurt. Not in anger, anyway. But that's why I said I'd be a private patient if I was dying.'

'So that is why you need the money?'

'No, no. I'm not going near a hospital. When the time comes, I'll die here. Even if I'm screaming with pain, at least the voyeurs won't get a look in, I'll have my dignity. I'll be like Frank Sinatra and Sid Vicious and Paul Anka and Dorothy Squires. I'll do it my way.'

I tried to interrupt by shaking my head violently, but Chris carried on talking as though she hadn't seen my face.

'If it's easier for you, take no notice of me, make out

I'm rambling. But I'm not. No, the reason I need money is nothing to do with me directly. Remember I told you I'd gone away last month? Well I hadn't, not in the way you thought. I went into hospital for all those tests on condition they told me the truth. And, to redress the balance, they were very good to me, the N.H.S., they kept their word. The consultant came to see me by himself when all the results were known. He sat on my bed and told me exactly what I told you this afternoon. The odd thing is that I remember the sister's annoyance because he was sitting on the bed as clearly as I remember his face and name and voice.'

She topped her glass up again.

'He was a kind man. I liked him. I implied that I'd have the operation but that I had to come home for a few days to sort things out, make arrangements. So I didn't actually have to discharge myself officially. Then I had this extraordinary urge to go and see Eva's grave. I had written down the name of the village ages ago, when you first told me, and I went straight there from the hospital, more or less. I felt too weak to go by train so I came back here to get some money out of my mattress and hired a minicab from that firm I always use for my clients. And you. They sent me that young chap Ray, so I didn't have to sit in the back. I always hate that, everyone knows you're buying your comfort. When we got there it was dark, so we stayed in that nice old pub. Separate rooms, more's the pity. He's the sort of young man I'd have ended up paying. There was a moment when I wondered about booking a double room, then I thought no, they don't know enough about cancer, I can't risk passing it on to him. And he would have shared a room with me, rather than hurt my feelings. A very rare young man. I was awfully tired. I had breakfast in bed, then he drove me round the corner to the churchyard. We were there nearly three hours, looking for her gravestone. He helped. When we couldn't find it, we went to the church itself. That beautiful Cotswold stone. I sat in the porch while he went to find someone. I was so tired I began to feel afraid . . . then he came back with the priest and this great big book. I told him the date and her name, because he was trying to be helpful, but I was angry with myself for apparently getting the name of the village wrong. I couldn't understand it.'

More gin; the last of it.

'But of course I hadn't got it wrong. There was Eva's name and the date and suddenly the priest remembered too. He told us to follow him and then there we were standing beside Eva's grave. I had forgotten how much taller than me she had been. I knew it was her grave because he told me; there was no other way of knowing. It was the only unmarked grave in the whole place.'

She put her emptying glass down and stumbled over towards me.

'He never gave her a headstone, Jock. Like a pauper's grave. Absolutely nothing to prove that she had ever existed. The priest was really wonderful. He took us to the presbytery and gave us coffee and sandwiches. I told him what I wanted and he made some phone calls and a man came to see me and suddenly everything began to be all right. Did you know they have catalogues for graves? It's being made now and they're going to let me know when it's ready. If it's too late for me, here is the priest's card. Promise me you will ring him and go and see it? They were so kind. We stayed the night at the presbytery and came back the next day. I paid a deposit and I've sent the rest off now. That's why I had to sell some things. Actually I didn't sell them. How could I possibly pass a sign with three balls at my time of life? And it seemed a quick and cheap way of making a will.

Here's the pawn ticket. Nothing of value to anyone but you. I'm sorry you'll have to pay, but thick paper and solicitors and sealing wax would probably have cost more.'

I felt pale with anger and grief at not grieving more, so remained silent. Chris, exhaustion coming out of her like a strobe light, finished her story.

'Jock and all his money. He never let Eva see me or write or telephone. He was ashamed of me and I suppose she let him be. He gave her all the things she had ever wanted materially, tried to buy her. He's not even worth our anger, Sadie. He never was. And believe me, Eva is going to have the most beautiful headstone possible. The priest rang this morning. It will be ready in about ten days. Don't lose that card. Father Keeffe, he's called.'

I spoke at last, my eyes focused on the empty gin bottle.

'What is the inscription?'

Chris put her arms round me again. 'Very simple. Just "Eva. Sister of Chris and aunt of Sadie. Too early seen: and known too late."'

She held me tighter.

'That's right. Aunt is what I had inscribed. I've always gone on about truth, I know, and now here I am ending my life on a lie. But a lie is sometimes nearer the truth than the truth. I believe now that, very occasionally, a lie can be justified.'

Fourteen

The telephone rang before I said anything, echoing in the room like the Lutine bell in stereo. Chris went to answer it, keeping her eyes on my face with the defiant innocence of a naughty child pleading not to be punished. She picked it up.

'Yes?' she said.

And, 'I'll tell her,' she said.

She put the receiver down and stood on the other side of the room, waiting for me to speak. Momentarily I was confused, feeling indeed as though Chris and Eva were both my children, their private supremacy battles nothing to do with me. Actually it was just that I was uncertain about the morals of lying on sanctified ground, and as soon as I realised just how much that doubt was being misunderstood, I held my hand out to her and said, 'It doesn't need justification. It is nearer the truth than the truth. You are the mother I could never reach before. Eva might have been a good aunt, someone glamorous floating on the periphery of a small child's world,' conscious as I spoke of how stilted and formal I sounded, not surprised Chris stayed where she was. 'Oh, Chris. Come here. Of course I don't mind. Shall I be honest about your lie? I was trying to think back to the convent and the missals and *The Illumination of Christ* and *Six O'Clock Saints*, wondering if there was any clause anywhere about extra time in Purgatory for being untruthful on consecrated ground.'

At last she was starting to smile and I remembered seeing that other look on her face once before, that fear of losing me, when she had originally told me how closely she was a part of my life. I went over to her and put my arms round her, but gently, not wanting to squeeze her too hard in case cancer was like toothpaste in a sealed tube.

I walked her across the room and sat her down. 'I'm just going to the off licence. We need more gin, and I'll get something for me too.'

She still couldn't absolutely stop looking at me. I put the front door on the latch and ran to the place, glad it was so near. I bought gin and lots of bottles of tonic for her and vodka and fresh orange for me. They had some small cigarettes, various kinds, and so I stocked up with them too, careless about the tar levels, now when it was too late. Back in the flat I went into the kitchen and organised our drinks, making both of them very strong and then guiltily diluting the alcohol with lots of ice. She looked stronger when I came back in, a little more erect.

'You can always blame me, say I was a silly old fool who didn't know what she was doing. And anyway, it was more a lie of omission.'

I said, to make sure that was her last word on the subject, 'Let's call it a lie of emission and be done with it,' and as she began to laugh she said, 'I should be so lucky.'

It wasn't easy to change the subject; we seemed to be surrounded by land mines in so many directions that there was danger in the mere exhalation of breath.

Her laugh turned into a cough and I threw her the cigarettes and a lighter I had bought. 'I hope you haven't wasted your money and got a refillable one.' The gin masquerading as bitterness was ugly and when she heard it she knew it, sucking an ice cube as if the numbness could make it unsaid.

I thought about offering her an easy, glib palliative and then decided that she neither wanted nor deserved it. She did look ill. If only I hadn't recently been so preoccupied with my own small world. She emptied her glass and I filled it for her again, another strong one, hoping that might help her sleep.

She got up and went over to the bureau before she drank a drop. She produced several envelopes, picked them up and waved them at me and then replaced them. 'Arrangements. I've made all my arrangements. They're roughly in order, I think. The top one tells you what to do when I actually die, who you ring first, things like that. Which crematorium and how much. There's another envelope with the exact money in it. I don't think one tips them. Well, you'll see what's in them, because they're all labelled. The rest of the money. The name and address of the pawnbroker in case you lose the ticket. That's paid up to date and I rang him and explained the situation, so he'll hold on to everything until he hears from you. The photographs of us as children. Oh, and there's another envelope with a list of some of my regulars who might ever be of any use to you. Most of them wouldn't be any fucking good to anyone if the way they fucked was anything to go by . . . sorry, I didn't mean to be so crass . . . but some were more special than others after all this time. There's a bank manager and a solicitor. I've rung them both, explained what's going on and told them I was giving you their numbers. Work numbers. Neither of them minded. The ones I've put a star by you might ring anyway, after my funeral, they're the ones who might be a bit upset. Oh, and there's my doctor. Surgeon, actually. I told you about him before, I think. He's retiring quite soon, but he has been very special. Came over from Hungary in '56. He'd already qualified there. Had to start all over again, learning the language, washing up, all sorts of jobs to pay his way through medical school. All that slog all over again. He was still a student when I first met him, but his English was very good by then. He would listen to people for hours, on buses, in coffee bars, on the street. I never charged him in the early days and then later, when he could afford it, I couldn't take the money, it seemed grubby somehow. He knows about you, all about you. If you ever need any kind of medical help, contact him, because if he can't help you himself he'll know someone who can. He was on holiday when we needed him before. He was very upset when he heard about all that. I still can't get his name right, but he came to see me a few days ago, solved a couple of problems for me, and he said not to worry, if someone rings up and asks for Dr Zhivago, he'll know it's you. He saw you once; you were leaving as he was arriving. Said he could see me in you. Old softy.'

How long her days must have been, that she could fill them with envelopes and efficiency and organisation like that. And why hadn't I been with her so that the echo in the envelopes of Eva would be less evident?

At last she picked up her glass again, and drank as though she was very thirsty. 'Sadie, there's only one thing I want you to know. Before all this, if I ever thought about death I was frightened, looking at it from behind. Now, like this, looking at it sideways, it's different, less frightening. Not smaller, but familiar. I think it must be like going to sleep, that's all. That's what you have to remember. All my bitterness or distress are focused on you, not seeing you. How happy you've made me. Now we don't talk about it any more? Oh God, I forgot to tell you. On the phone, earlier, Tim.

Some problem. They've been sent home. So, off you go. Now that I've seen you, everything is all right for me.'

And then the memory of Tim's deception came back to me. To cope with what was happening to Chris I had to be able to cope with that.

'Look, if I go now, I can pick up some things and be back here in the morning to look after you. I don't need a cab, I've got the Mini. I'll load it up and be back tomorrow. Still lots of questions.'

'Sometimes there aren't any answers. 'Bye, 'bye, my darling Sadie. You have made me happy.'

'See you in the morning.'

'Goodbye. Much love.'

I had hidden the spare key in my pocket, in case she was able to have a good long sleep.

'A lie can be justified. Even a lie of omission,' Tim said, his grief so palpable that I had only heard his words dimly until I looked away from his face. So now I was hearing him, but what I was seeing was the photostat of the form from the fertility clinic on the table between us like the Berlin Wall.

'Go ahead then, justify it,' I said in a voice so spiteful that neither of us recognised it.

'I only said it can be justified. Not that I could do it. But I'll try.'

I had never heard a silence so full of effort before. I could have helped him but my day with Chris had turned me into an empty first aid box, and when he did speak fear cracked his familiar fluency.

'Telling you would have meant breaking your heart with my own guilt . . . thought if you could go on hoping . . . even hoped they might be wrong . . . doctors do make mistakes . . . thought I'd hurt you enough . . . went to see them alone and they said what I was asking wasn't ethical . . . I said smashing your life wasn't ethical either, if there was a choice . . . I begged them, pleaded, eventually . . . cried . . . they got so embarrassed then that they said O.K., they wouldn't tell you, they'd maintain the pretence . . . that's why I always came with you even when you didn't want me to . . . the terror that one day, if I wasn't there, they'd tell you the truth; today would happen . . . and of course I paid them, they said they couldn't do that on the National Health, you'd have to become a private patient . . . '

That shocked me more than some of the other things I'd heard that day.

'You mean they don't lie on the National Health? Is that why they keep building more private hospitals?'

Tim said, 'I think they probably do anything if you pay them.'

I stood up: I couldn't think of anything else to do.

'Tim, I'm going to stay with Chris tonight. Sort my mind out. Let's talk tomorrow when I've taken it all in. And thank you. For not lying about the lie.'

I picked up my bag. And then he said it, the one thing I hoped I would never hear again.

'Sadie, I did it because I love you.'

And that's how I came to find Chris still alive but unconscious, empty pill bottles scattered around her, the mahogany Madonna in a thin paper bag with my name on it on the bed beside her, only three hours after I had left. Despite all that gin she didn't die until the middle of the following night. I lay beside her on the bed all that time and there was no staring or gossiping or noise. I didn't fiddle about with machines or thermometers. There'd be time for that when I called the ambulance when it was all over. I just lay beside her, warming her with my body, giving her her dignity when she had wanted it, when it had some value.

So, in a way, both of us paid for Eva's headstone. Chris with money and me with my complicity in the lie that eventually made me agree that lies can perhaps be justified if the liar's need is great enough.

Chris had indeed made all the arrangements. There was just one thing she hadn't known, that if you die at home by your own hand there has to be an inquest; so I had to go and tell them what Chris had told me about her illness. I didn't tell them I'd been there with her, waiting for it to happen, this death that she had planned and deserved far more than the alternative. I lied, said I had arrived to find her like that. I was shocked at how easy it was, how much simpler than telling the truth would have been.

The coroner agreed that Chris could have been dead when he had returned his verdict of 'suicide while the balance of the mind was disturbed', which was so ludicrous that I wanted to look up and wink at Chris.

Then there was a strike at the crematorium: Chris would have loved that, being involved in something the newspapers labelled 'disgusting' in one brief paragraph under the Page Three girl.

When the coffin finally slid silently through the curtains towards the man-made hellfire we're supposed to spend our lives defying, I hoped that Chris was less aware of the hypocrisy of the world than I was. Even lay schools preach the doctrine of choice, but where was it now? No other set of curtains opened on to privileged heavenly sunshine; it was fire or nothing.

Tim was waiting for me in the car outside. I had rung him immediately Chris died and he had wanted to come with me to the funeral. It had never occurred to me not to ring him; at that time Chris dying seemed so very much more final than my inability to conceive. And I needed him.

As I got into the car next to him, I carried on thinking about that solitary set of curtains, talked about them to Tim because it was easier than talking about anything else.

'Probably just as well,' I concluded. 'Imagine how awful it would be if the survivors were given an inkling at the moment of departure that the deceased had led a life less or more blameless than had been imagined. Priests whisked into hell, murderers transported straight to the Elysian Fields.'

'That's democracy for you,' Tim replied, changing gear at the lights, 'and think of the bribery and corruption that would go on if there was a real choice. They'd do anything if you paid them.'

'That's what you said about private doctors.'

'What?'

'I think they probably do anything if you pay them.'

And so I buried Chris, dreading coming to the end of having something to do, so that my grief would be able only to turn back on itself, crackling backwards and forwards between sensation and articulation like a two-way radio with faulty microphones.

Fifteen

Tim stayed with me as long as he could. They were generous with compassionate leave and he was generous with his compassion, anticipating my needs and moods, loving, gentle and there. We made love with a less desperate urgency than before, and not nearly so often now that it was only for our mutual pleasure and not to create a small image of ourselves. The numbness that Chris's absence precipitated made me forgive his lie about the baby for the time being. It was easier for me to believe his explanation than to challenge it continually. Otherwise it would have been impossible for me to go on loving him or to believe that he did really love me, and without that giving and receiving of love my life would not have been tolerable.

I could not speak of the desolation and loneliness I felt about Chris, because it was the part of my life from which he had been excluded. When Tim was home I was entirely his and he had never known quite how important my time with her had been, or how close we had been. The odd thing was his total failure to ask me anything about her, because if he had once said, Tell me who she was, I would have told him everything he wanted to know. I would even have told him about Eva and Jock as well, for now he was all I had in the world and I felt able at last to put right my lie of long ago in the motorway café, so that I could share my whole life with him as an equal. He had admitted to his lies; I longed to admit to mine. But he never asked.

I was curious about his absolute lack of curiosity and not long before he had to return to work I said so. He gave a mock frown and said, 'I know, isn't it awful? I used to ask so many questions, and then when sometimes I got your answers, I stopped. It worried me for ages until I realised what it was that made me lose it, it was like losing an extra sense. Curiosity killed the cat, and it was killing me.'

'But satisfaction brought it back.'

'That's how I knew I wasn't a cat. I felt guilty, privileged almost, because I hadn't suffered. I had parents, a happy childhood, security. I thought if I stopped asking questions that security would rub off on you, that you would absorb that and share it and imagine that it was yours too. Perhaps I was wrong, perhaps you should make me suffer?'

And that was the end of the conversation because he started to undo my blouse and kiss my breasts. He picked me up and carried me into the bedroom where the daylight was still flooding through the window on to the bed. He did my blouse up again and sat looking at me whilst his fingers played on my breasts, circling round and round my nipples across the thin silk, brushing one finger over them and then moving away again. Then he sat me up against the bedhead so that my breasts were bigger and fuller and almost too big for his hands to hold. And still he tantalised me, watching my face with a slight smile, knowing that as long as I was so full of desire I would not be able to register pain as well deep down in my belly. I kept trying to reach out for him but he wouldn't let me touch him. 'Not yet. This is for you. I want to see your eyes change colour. I want you to remember this while I am away, want you to remember what I can do to you, how much I love you.' I have no sense of time, how long he kept me on that edge, but when finally he slowly undid my buttons again, the patch of daylight had moved away from the bed towards the Madonna. Even after he had undone the buttons he continued to touch me through the fabric, easing it little by little away from the middle until finally when the room was almost dark I felt the cold air for a moment on my nipples and then his mouth and his hands covered them so that they were warm. Only then did he let me reach out for him and at the same time he unzipped my jeans as well. He was harder and bigger than I had ever known him. I have absolutely no idea how long we went on for. All I do know is that when we had finished the room was in total darkness. It was the best fuck we had ever had, and the most unselfish and loving I had ever known Tim. For hours all he had done was give me pleasure, and if I had said thank you it would have spoiled it for both of us. We lay together in exhausted silence, limp, drained and soaking wet. And the very best part of all was that he didn't fall asleep on top of me. But. As my body gradually returned to its more precise outline, I came to my senses and thought that if Chris was watching me through the old star-eaten blanket of the sky she would probably be rather pleased, so I turned towards Tim, who was lying there smiling and said, 'There's a terrible smell of fish and chips. Would you like a cup of tea?'

He kissed me on my cheek. 'I've got a better idea. Why don't I go out and get some fish and chips? It will give the aroma some respectability.'

And so that's what we did, ate fish and chips out of the newspaper, watching the late night movie. We didn't bath until later, savouring the confusion of smells. Then, deep, dreamless sleep, the part of the day I still looked forward to most. The next morning we made love again, but the more perfunctory kind, the early morning blow job. As it ended the telephone rang. Tim answered it and then said, 'Wait a minute, I'll just go to the other phone, this line is crackly,' and he got out of bed and padded into the sitting room. He shut the door behind him and I dozed off again.

He woke me up a couple of hours later with a cup of tea and a look of real distress. I didn't notice it at first, his misery, because the tea was so good and less salty, if I'm honest, than spunk. I smiled at him when I had finished without properly noticing his face, smiling more at his outline. 'I suppose there's no chance of another cup is there?'

And then I forgot all about my thirst as I registered my husband's stance. He was leaning against the wall my side of the bed with one hand over his face to hide what seemed to be tears, except that Tim never cried. I jumped out of bed and pulled his hand away, and his face was wet. I looked at the rest of him, hoping to see that he had been in the shower and was just wet all over, but he was fully dressed in dry clothes.

'Tim, what's happened, what's wrong?'

He looked at me and now it was his eyes that had changed colour. He put his hand out towards me, but it fell to his side before he actually touched me. I passed him a tissue and he wiped his eyes and blew his nose and his irises faded back to their more familiar grey-blue.

He came and sat on the bed beside me, but not touching me. 'Sadie, when I came back early, when Chris died, I didn't tell you the real reason. You'd been told about no baby, there was the funeral to organise, you had enough to cope with. I've been here with you for a month now and even to me it seems a long time ago. But there was a diving accident; I was lucky but a friend of mine was killed. It happened just before I got back up there. All I could do was go to the funeral, I was too late to try and help save him. Not that I would have been able to do anything, but there will always be that slight niggle of doubt, and if only, and perhaps. Anyway, they've closed that diver's bell down until they've found out exactly what went wrong. That phone call just now was from head office. I'm going to say this next bit quickly. I've got to go out to the Gulf. Tomorrow. For at least one month. Maybe two. Wives aren't allowed. Even if they were, there'd be no point because we're never on land. I tried to get out of it but they just said, "Barlow, we need you there. You decided to join the firm, knowing that you go where we choose to send you. You shouldn't do your job so well if you're going to pussyfoot around like a virginal prick-teaser. And there is no one else with your experience. Your flight leaves at eleven a.m. tomorrow. Your ticket is waiting for you at Heathrow." And they're paying me so much money that we can buy a house in the country. And then when I'm back we can adopt a couple of babies.'

I couldn't look at him; we sat side by side like two catatonics. I looked at the wall and all I could see was Chris carved on a tombstone with three balls in her hand. When Tim had first spoken I had been afraid, hoping that I was deaf, but then I felt a curious relief. If he was away I would be able to be with Chris again, allowed to grieve and mourn and remember, and then when he returned perhaps I would have made sense of Eva and Chris. I would have answered sooner if he hadn't talked about adopting a child. I didn't want someone else's child, I wanted my own, something that grew inside me, was fed by my body, my blood, a Holy Communion child that was also part of Chris and Eva and my father. If I had a baby growing inside me I could call it something different every day, secretly, privately, something shared only by the two of us, but a part of all that was me.

I spoke to Tim, looking only at Chris's image on the wall. 'I think it's a marvellous idea. I'm very proud of you, that they chose you. Two months is such a short time out of our lives. And we can write, and I can catch up on all the work I haven't done and I can decorate the flat so that when you come back we can really start a new life. Before you I never needed anyone. I'll be all right. You taught me that needing people was important, and you made me believe that it was important, that I mustn't confuse it with pity. Do you remember me saying, ages ago, before we got married, that I was never going to need anyone because if I ever did learn to lean on someone I'd end up believing that I wouldn't overbalance, and then suddenly *wham*, I'd be flat on my back because my leaning post turned out to have Dutch Elm disease? And you said that Dutch Elm disease wouldn't stand a chance, and anyway, you needed to be needed to make you feel whole, and I didn't even have to say it or even to think it, just sometimes feel it and you'd know? Well, in the end that happened, and it's not going to go away just because you are. Come on. We'd better start packing.'

Tim, expecting objections from me, was a little bit put out that I agreed so readily; he was unsure how to react and watched me to see if I really did mean what I had said. It must have been obvious from the way that I looked back at him that I was speaking the truth.

'Won't you miss me at all?'

'Of course I will, you don't have to ask that. All I'm saying is that when you come back, that's when our life can begin properly. All the old ghosts will have gone and it will be just you and me. The books I'm supposed to have read are mounting up, and maybe I can give it up, the job, when you come back. It'll be hot out there, so let's sort out what you've got and what we must buy this afternoon. Which suitcase do you think you'll need?'

Tim wanted to say something else, I think, about us and our future together, but I had switched off, was back in the memory of packing school trunks at short notice, back in the world where feelings were not allowed to exist, knowing how to communicate that coldness. It was as though I was Eva and Tim her unwanted child. By ten o'clock that night everything was ready for his departure.

We didn't make love in case the memory of it intruded too strongly on the next eight weeks. But we did talk about some of our many happy times together. Tim reminded me that I had once said no other couple could spend as much time making love as we did, because otherwise the country would be in an even worse mess than it was already; Tim had laughed and said, 'What do you think an economic recession is, then? An increase in the withdrawal method because nobody can afford to go all the way any more?'

But all that was a memory, not a reality. We lay stiffly in the bed, careful not to touch each other, a sacrifice to the Arab world where men were men and women were behind veils. And then we obviously slept, for the alarm call began our divorce proceedings.

As Tim was packing his last few bits and pieces I sat and watched him, terrified of what I was going to have to recognise as my reality without Chris. As long as he was here there were times when I could pretend that Chris and Eva had never happened. I asked Tim for an address where I could contact him if necessary, something I had never done before. He said he couldn't give me the exact address but wrote down the name of the head office over here and said that they would forward any mail to him and as soon as he knew something more definite he would let me know. He tucked the slip of paper into the mirror in the bathroom.

The car to take him to the airport honked outside. 'I wish you didn't have to go,' I said, not meaning to.

'What's all this then?' Tim said uncertainly, 'I thought you enjoyed the rest.'

I sensed that he wished I would send him off as I usually did, with a sexual innuendo and a joke, but I could only remain serious, not answer his smile.

'Tim, when you said you wished I would make you suffer, did you mean it?'

'Only in the interests of equality, and as long as it isn't going to hurt me.'

The joke fell flat. The car hooted again.

'Well, goodbye then. My Sadie.'

'Goodbye. My Tim.'

He got as far as the front door and then came back. I thought he was going to kiss my mouth, but he dropped his head lower and kissed each of my breasts in turn. 'Look after my babies for me. Two months isn't very long.'

'No. Time for two periods, that's all.'

And then he was gone and I had nothing to do for two months except kill time. I drank endless cups of coffee and played two tracks from two records over and over again. 'A Little Bit of Emotion' from the Kinks' 'Low Budget' and 'Guilt' from Marianne Faithfull's 'Broken English', wondering about the random chromosome which had genetically determined that I should have such an abundance of both. Then I grimaced at my egocentric curiosity, saluting the XX factor that had made me a woman.

I tidied the flat, cleaning it meticulously, washing down the paintwork so that if I did actually get round to painting it the groundwork would already have been done.

By the time I had finished I was too exhausted even to have a bath, and I still didn't know what the time was. I lay on the top of the bed, a niggling thought that I had forgotten something filling my head with silence as I looked at the two Madonnas which were so obviously a pair, since they were looking towards each other, holding their own babies so close to them that only the mothers' eyes met. I was on the verge of remembering this thing that I knew was important when the telephone rang. I didn't want to pick it up because it wouldn't be airborne Tim and it wouldn't be Chris, so I let it ring, hoping it would stop. It didn't.

'Hello.'

An American voice. Female.

'Hello. Could I speak to Tim please?'

'I'm sorry. He's not here. He's gone abroad.'

'Oh, of course. He's gone already, has he? To the Gulf?'

'Yes.'

'Well, if you hear from him, could you please give him a message from me?'

If I hear from him? If? I was silent.

'Hello, are you still there?'

'I'm here.'

'Good. If you hear from him, could you tell him that I rang?'

'If you tell me who I is. And not if. When.'

'Do you have a pen? It is really important that he gets this message.'

'I have a good memory. I won't forget what you say if it really is important.'

'O.K., then. Could you tell him that Margie rang. Thank him so very much for everything. Tell him that I'm just off to Heathrow, I'm going back home to the States.'

'Fine. I'll tell him that. O.K.?'

'No, no, I haven't come to the important bit. Tell him I got the result this morning. I'm definitely pregnant. That's what he will really want to know. And thank him again and give him much love.'

'I'll tell him,' I said and hung up.

Margie. What a fucking stupid name. If he had to dabble in cholesterol Flora would have been more acceptable.

One of the Madonnas fell off the wall.

Sixteen

I don't remember the next few days; it was as though I had died. I had become deaf and dumb, was left only with my sight, so that the bedroom wall was like a cinema screen on to which I was able to project all the images in my head that made so little sense; I was like a latter-day Miss Marples, showing the slides over and over again, looking for the common denominator, the solution. One-breasted Eva. Chris and her quisling uterus. My two breasts and superfluous womb. Tim and his spunk that I could not fertilise. An American belly great with the jelly baby Tim had made me dissolve. Him calling my breasts his babies.

It didn't come into my head immediately; merely, one day I came back to life and remembered Tim saying that perhaps I should make him suffer in the interests of equality and as long as it didn't hurt him. It was so simple, so obvious, that I wondered why it had taken me so long to think of it. I switched off the slide projector. No time to waste.

'I thought you did anything if you were paid. I'm not asking for this on the N.H.S.,' I stuttered to the first private consultant I saw, surprised by his anger.

'I think you will find that most of us prefer to leave mutilation to drunken drivers,' was his cold dismissal as he gestured to his receptionist to show me out.

I persevered, becoming a justifiably accomplished liar in the process. At first I had tried to tell the truth, but nobody seemed to understand me so I gradually slipped in little lies, and some of them appeared to help. Even then I was cautious, for they were too easy and I kept waiting for them to become difficult and dangerous. But they didn't. I cannot remember how many surgeons I saw; they are a blur of varying ages, sizes, fees and nationalities. Some were angry, some distressed and shocked and the remainder suggested psychiatric help.

So then I went to the library and took out some medical books and locked myself in the flat, preparing a really watertight case incorporating truth and untruth in equal proportions. Perhaps I also stayed at home longer than necessary because I was afraid that I might succeed.

I made another appointment and as I put on my jacket I felt in the pocket and found Chris's bundle of envelopes. The thing I had been trying to remember when the mother of Tim's child had rung had been the pawn ticket. But there were the other envelopes too and why hadn't I thought of it before? 'Anything you want, just ring him. He promised that if ever you need help he'll give it to you. Remember that. Dr Zhivago. He promised me and he doesn't break his promises.'

I rang his number from a call box on my way back from the pawnbrokers. He would see me immediately.

His consulting rooms were in one of those small inaccessible streets near Shepherd Market and it took me ages to find somewhere to park. In the end I left the Mini on a yellow line and hoped for the best. The carrier bags containing Chris's life were safely locked in the boot.

I was shown into his room immediately and he stood up and smiled at me as if we were old friends, although what he said belied this. 'So. You are Sadie. Anyone who could make Chris as happy as you did is a friend of mine. Sit down, have a drink and tell me about her . . . '

'You do know that she is dead, don't you?'

'I gave her the pills. The pain would have become intolerable . . . I loved her. Like you loved her. I gave her what she wanted. I hope it didn't take too long.'

I told him everything he wanted to know and was very moved by his reactions, his face, his obvious sense of loss. It was so good to have someone to share her with. I even told him about the cremation and the go slow and his eyes watered fractionally but only as if they needed new washers.

'Did you know,' he said, when I had finished speaking, 'how many times I asked her to marry me? She always said no of course. Except that last time I saw her. Then she said, "It's too late for marriage, but there are other promises just as binding. If ever Sadie needs you, be there." So. I'm here. You're here. I would never break a promise I made to Chris, whatever the consequences. Is this a social visit, or can I do something for you?'

'I think you should decide that,' I said, paused, lit a cigarette, and began to talk. I talked for a long time, giving him no opportunity to interrupt. When I began he was facing me, and by the time I had finished his swivel chair had turned round so that all I saw was his back, his silhouette against the window. There was a long, long silence. Long enough for me to smoke two cigarettes down to the filter tip.

His stillness gave me absolutely no indication of what his reaction to my request might be. It was the spin of a coin; it was also my last chance. I lit a third cigarette and he turned gradually back so I could begin to see his face.

I think it was his sadness that made me realise that he was going to say yes before he actually said it.

That and a kind of understanding of what it meant to

be terribly alone. He didn't want to agree with what I had said, but his own recognition of isolation and his love for Chris made it impossible for him to say no.

When he did finally speak, he was totally professional and efficient and practical. There was no emotion, no begging me to reconsider.

He rang for his nurse, his chaperone.

'Would you show Mrs Barlow into the examination room please?'

In there I stripped to the waist and the nurse told him that I was ready. He came in and examined my breasts unhurriedly, but he did not have Tim's touch and I was not at all embarrassed. I winced slightly each time he touched the left one and he prodded harder so that my demonstration of pain became real.

Then he left the cubicle and returned to his office. The nurse went with him. I heard him make a couple of telephone calls, but I didn't hear what he said, just the low rumble of his voice. I wasn't sure whether I was supposed to get dressed again or not, so I remained on the hard couch half-naked.

Then I heard him calling out to the nurse that she could go home early and would she switch the phone through to the answering service. A longish silence and then I heard her shouted goodnight and the slam of the front door.

Dr Zhivago came back into the confessional.

'Right. I've booked you a bed for next Tuesday. I'll give you all the details when we get back in the other room. I just have to make a small incision now, under a local anaesthetic. All right? Be ready in a couple of minutes.'

'You're not going to do it while I'm still awake?' I almost shrieked in fear.

'No, no, no. Just a small incision and a couple of

stitches, so it looks as though I've done a biopsy. Otherwise they'll wonder why I'm not doing one there, d'you see?'

'Can't you say you're doing it because I have mastitis?'

'I must say you've done your research very thoroughly. There are surgeons who remove breasts for chronic and extreme mastitis, but I'm not one of them. Even if you did have it. I will do what you want, but it must be for a more acceptable reason. Right. Little prick coming. Just to freeze it . . . There, that didn't hurt, did it? By the time I've got my scalpel and some sutures it'll be numb.'

And so I took the first irrevocable step. He was quite right. It didn't hurt. I got dressed and stood up slowly as though my body was suddenly immensely heavy, which was odd because next week it would be considerably lighter. I wondered how much a breast weighed.

Dr Zhivago was filling in forms and slips of paper. I sat opposite him again. When he had finished he handed me a slip of paper.

'There you are. The address of the hospital, your number, what you need to take in with you. How are you off for money? I cannot arrange for you to go into a private hospital free. I don't want any money from you, of course, but the hospital fees alone will come to about eight hundred pounds. Can you raise that?'

'Yes,' I lied. Then I said 'Yes' again, truthfully this time, for I would sell the car. The pawnbroker had taken the last of my own earned money, and it didn't seem morally acceptable to use money from our joint account.

'I'll see you on Wednesday then.'

'I thought you said Tuesday . . . '

'You go in on Tuesday. I operate on Wednesday. I officially retire on Friday.' Abruptly he switched from his earlier professionalism back to the man who had loved Chris.

'So I reached you just in time?'

He rubbed his hand over his eyes.

'I'll never know that. I only know what I promised Chris, but I do partly understand why you are asking me to do this. I knew about Eva and Chris. I know about your abortion and the fertility clinic visits, but I didn't, of course, know that your husband had deceived you either in withholding information from you or in impregnating another woman. Certainly the generally accepted idea is that men's infidelities commence at or around the time their women are in hospital being treated for entirely female problems. If they're gynaecological, many men seem to feel women's esoteric pleasures must be punished by betrayal and infidelity. But if the disease or illness is of a nature that men and women both experience, then of course fidelity and solicitude are usual, indeed preferable, for as ye sow so shall ye reap.'

'You're very cynical.'

'Not without reason. This job . . . makes you understand women, love them sometimes . . . but it also makes it harder to like my own sex. I've never thought of revenge before, even though I know that that is only part of it, that you are trying to make sense of other things, but part of me knows that it can be justified. I'm doing this for you and many other women as well. All the same, if I was not retiring, I don't know how I would choose between ethics and loyalty to Chris. But I am.'

'Thank you. Thank you very much indeed. I'll see you next week then?'

'On Wednesday.' He shook my hand – looking sad and old.

Back at home I busied myself with arranging some of Chris's things in the flat. Other objects, the notes, the photographs, I put in a suitcase under the bed. Most of the cash she had left me I paid into our account, knowing that it would be unfair to use it for this. Selling the car was the obvious choice, since that had come from Jock in the first place, via the Mercedes. It seemed right that he should pay, for I still sometimes dreamed that if it had not been for him Eva would have spoken to me of her love and pride. I also wondered at times if Jock was not perhaps entirely to blame, if separate bedrooms so early in their marriage had been her choice and not his, but I pushed those thoughts away.

Now that the decision was taken out of my hands, I found it much easier to be normal and efficient. I sold the car for a thousand pounds, knowing that I could have got more for it but knowing too that there was more than enough in the building society to buy several more cars. I corrected the proofs that had piled up during the past few weeks and delivered them to the publisher's with a note saying that I was going on holiday and would let them know when I was back. It was Monday now and I checked through the list of things I was supposed to take in with me the next day, buying what I hadn't got and packing it all so that there would be no rush the next day.

I went to bed early and fell almost immediately into a deep and dreamless sleep.

Seventeen

I put the telephone down very fast and wiped the receiver with a tissue, as though by preserving anonymity and removing my fingerprints the decision was not mine, I could deny that I had ever been in that call box. And anyway the news contained in the telegram itself was so shocking that by the time the head office in London had contacted Tim in the Gulf it was unlikely that anyone would think of checking the source. I simply felt it was unfair to put that telegram on our own phone bill. Nevertheless, I felt safer when my hands were empty, receiverless.

Three days at least before he could hope to be back; three days of no longer feeling married; three days of special danger. And that was without the more available and familiar dangers I was inviting by entering the hospital in front of me.

In the distance Big Ben chimed eleven times and I looked at my watch, knowing that it would be wrong. I double checked with my last 5p, still annoyed that no one had told me that calls had gone up overnight, and failing to understand how they could change all the money slots without repairing the vandalised phones at the same time. The one-two-three lady sounded tired and rather hoarse. And according to her, Big Ben was thirty seconds slow. But some institutions should never be challenged so I made my watch thirty seconds slow as well. As I left the call box I noticed that the hospital opposite looked totally different now that I was not seeing it through glass. Smaller, cleaner, safer. I crossed the road.

Inside it didn't seem at all like a hospital, even a private one. Without the ether smells of childhood nightmares there seemed nothing to be afraid of. It diminished the experience somehow.

A porter welcomed me in three languages, none of them English. He jerked his head and his uniform made me obey and follow him to a day ward on the ground floor.

He led me past a vacuuming orderly towards a kind of dormitory where the beds were out of alignment with the curtainless curtain rails because there were far too many of them. Young women were lying on most of them, some conscious, others not, although it was hard to tell the difference since fear is itself an anaesthetic.

Another uniform approached, this time wearing a frilly cap, and puzzled rather than indifferent. 'Hello. Sorry if I look vague. I thought all my girls were here. What's your name?' Drowning in a sense of déjà-vu, remembering trying to make a curtain ring look gold and as though it belonged on my finger, I nearly invented an Arabic name to protect the innocent and obviate my own mistake. Tim's mistake.

The girl with the vacuum cleaner came closer and it was possible to imagine that the machine she was using was the very same as that being used to Hoover all those nice fertile young wombs back into submission.

On the second floor they seemed to be waiting for me, Sister and her girls. I was shown to my private-room-with-bath and I gratefully flopped into the one comfortable chair it contained. Curtains, cushion and bedspread were all made of the same swirly orangy-yellow fabric and as I blinked my eyes it was possible to imagine myself to be sitting in the middle of an egg.

I smiled because I didn't ever cry. 'I never had children really.' It was such an odd thing to have said that I was grateful when an alien thermometer was thrust under my tongue.

One more memory forced its way towards me. It got as far as sepia before some natural acid bleached it back to oblivion. I had once offered to help Tim with his accounts. In gratitude for his acceptance of this offer I had bought myself a calculator, but had ended up doing all the sums in my head as well to make sure that they were right. I had finally learned to trust the black plastic but then someone had told me that as the batteries ran down it started giving the wrong answers. So I'd put new batteries in the damned thing and still ended up doing the sums on my own as well. Tim had laughed at first and repeated the story to friends, and that had been fine as long as his arm was around me, but when someone I had not met before had said, quite recently, 'Hi, I gather you double check the silicon chip,' in a loud voice at a quiet party, I had felt ashamed when people laughed.

'I find it impossible,' I had said, too harshly, 'to trust a silicon chip in the face of the evidence and the precedents set by trusting a human being.'

'One mustn't even trust the post any more, must one? Gravity will be the next to go, I shouldn't wonder,' our hostess had trilled, and had given me a bigger drink.

An accountant had done the accounts since then. The last drop of bleach; and then the nurse was saying, 'How will you be paying your account?'

'With the wages of sin if I'm lucky,' I said.

As the nurse started to laugh I said, 'Why am I so afraid?'

I remembered how on my first night with Tim I had

put the light on and without the dark I had no longer been so afraid. 'I am not afraid of anything,' I had heard myself saying.

This was untrue now. I was afraid of the things Tim could do to my body. I was afraid of the long journey back to solitude now that we had travelled so far together. Afraid of him going. Afraid of him staying. Afraid of him loving me, of him not loving me; of exposing too much of myself and too little. Afraid of his lies, afraid of his truths; afraid that I might not know the difference. How I wish that when I flicked the light on on that long-ago night, the bulb had blown, that the room had remained invisible. My fear is so enormous that if I speak in the dark it is only to tell the truth. I must be afraid of the truth.

I went into the little bathroom to provide the requested specimen of urine. My period had finished the day before, but I seemed to be still bleeding a little. As I gave the jug of pee to the nurse I said, 'I'm sorry, but do you have any sanitary towels? Don't worry, you won't have to send me home, it's the last dregs. Probably just God reminding me that I'm still vaguely female.'

'Don't. Please don't. I'll get you a couple,' and she left the room, not smiling now. I went back into the bathroom to get undressed and when I came back into the room there were two enormous sanitary towels on the bed. Maternity size.

I answered all the questions she asked me for her admissions book, and then she helped me unpack my few things. It still looked like an anonymous hospital room and I wished I had bought myself some flowers or a plant to make it look as though I was less alone.

By the time evening came boredom was making me feel tired and that, combined with the sleeping pill they gave me, really knocked me out. They woke me up early the next morning, for I was the first one on the list. I was asked to have a shower and shave under my left arm, but it seemed important to do both as though it were routine, the night before a summer holiday. As I came back into my room from the bathroom the same nurse I had seen yesterday was waiting with a hospital gown and an injection. She wasn't hurrying me, just hovering, sympathetic, curious.

'I'll just have a last pee,' I said.

'Oh Christ, hang on, I need another specimen. Good job you reminded me. Just to double check. Are you still bleeding? And can you go in this jug?'

'My aim is true, if nothing else.'

The nurse took the shaving things away; I peed. Most of it seemed to go on my hand but the warmth was curiously comforting and there was enough left to test.

I took off my own nightdress in front of the mirror and hesitated a moment before putting on the theatre gown. I looked at my breasts. They looked the same as they always had, nothing about the left one to indicate that it might be in jeopardy. I wondered whether Tim would mind losing one of his babies as much as I had minded losing mine; whether the loss would make him as sterile as it had made me. The gown was not the kind I had had at that last hospital, with so many strings I could have hung myself; this one was even more complicated, its simplicity negated by strips of Velcro whose destination was unclear. The nurse came back.

'Your pee's O.K. No trace of alcohol. It never shows the good things of life. One day they'll invent a theatre gown that doesn't require a map and a compass. Here, let me help you.'

I wasn't thinking of babies any more; I was becoming one as the nurse dressed me and led me back to my bed. The injection stung a bit and, absurdly, I wished I could cry, but my tear ducts had been blocked long ago by crystals of salt from all the forbidden weeping of early childhood.

Then I thought of Tim, wondered where he was and imagined my woozy feeling to be a memory of the moments after sex. But it was only the Omnopon and Scopolamine, and obediently I fell asleep, no memories like incontinent stains clouding my vision of infinity. I barely awoke when they lifted me on to the theatre trolley and wheeled me to the anaesthetic room.

The gowns and masks and unresponsive eyes were the same as when they had taken my baby away finally and now, as then, someone swabbed the back of my hand and said, 'Little prick coming.' I should be so lucky.

The morning passed. Banks opened, girls bought bikinis, dole queues lengthened, babies were born, cars nearly crashed, people made love, the cost of living went up, children went hungry; an average London morning.

Back in my bed I came round briefly from my anaesthetic and felt my left breast. I mistook the padding for flesh and, content, slept again. This was a good trip. Nothing hurt. Nothing had changed. And anyway I was still asleep.

Each time I thought I was waking up I was knocked out by another little prick, followed by the familiar stinging sensation. The grass wasn't only greener; it was also home grown.

The night passed. Banks were raided, girls vowed to diet, Social Security officers slept in complacent indifference, babies died, cars crashed, people made war, adults went hungry; an average London night.

Eighteen

When I woke up the morning after my operation I felt oddly triumphant, as though I had just coined the word equality, its meaning more precisely defined than before. The physical pain heightened the triumph as its absence would have diminished it. Even the smaller discomfort of the drip in my arm deserved recognition.

Dr Zhivago came in, Sister in attendance.

Perhaps he was a frustrated actor, for he played his part brilliantly, adopting the sympathy and bonhomie you would expect from an uncle you had never met but with whom you had exchanged Christmas cards.

'I'm sorry, my dear, but I have had to remove your breast. A simple mastectomy. I've left you the glands under your arm, though, you won't be numb there.'

And 'Thank you,' I said, 'that's nice.'

'Everything went well. According to plan.' He raised his eyebrows slightly on the last phrase, as if to emphasise it. I looked at him at the exact moment that he looked from me to Sister. His voice was even as he said, 'The drip can come down after that saline is through. And I'll be back in tomorrow.'

'I'll ring you when the path. report comes through shall I, Sir?'

'No need, m'dear. It's being sent to me direct. I'll take her notes with me too. Everything in one place.'

Sister was shocked. This was not ethical. But, too, this was Sir. Perhaps he'd been caught in the rush hour traffic. Nevertheless, they did normally mention the word malignant when they talked to their post-op patients for the first time, even if they couldn't say cancer. Perhaps he would ask her to do that for him; he was a very busy man. She started humming 'Nearer my God to Thee' as he looked back at me and repeated, 'According to plan. Drip down this afternoon. All right?'

I, not all right, wanting the lesser pain of the drip to counteract the greater pain of the drainage bottles and the lost breast to last longer, was about to speak when Sister said, 'By the way, Mrs Barlow, your husband telephoned from abroad. He'll be here as soon as he can to see you. I'll be back in a minute.' The door closed behind them and my physical pain receded absolutely. My body seemed momentarily whole and perfect again compared with the jagged, fractured disintegration inside my head. In all the planning, the decision, the danger and the horror of what I had done I had never thought beyond the moment when Tim would get the telegram. The idea of seeing him had not been something possible to focus on.

Sister came back in with an injection.

'Sorry to keep you waiting, love. Your surgeon hasn't had a patient on my ward before. We must be going up in the world. He usually uses the Wellington or King Edward VII for Officers.'

'Well, I may not be an officer, but I'm half a gentleman now.'

'Now, now. Don't let's have any silly talk like that. Don't misunderstand me, you've had every woman's nightmare while you're awake, but being bitter isn't going to help. Maybe later. But not yet. We've got to get you feeling better physically first. Cry if you like, but don't be bitter. We can cope with tears but not that.

Some of my nurses are very young. They get upset.'

'Of course. I'm sorry. It's very selfish of me.'

'Good girl. Here's something for your pain. No, it's all right, don't try and turn over with all these tubes, I'll give it to you in your thigh.' She turned the covers back. 'We'll have to fatten you up. Prick coming. There. All right?'

Half an hour ago I would have rejected any analgesic, wanting to remember the pain, experience it indelibly so that I could recreate it in the future at will, a gift Tim would never know I had given him. Now I welcomed it, unable to cope with two such different agonies.

'Thank you, Sister. What did my husband say when he rang?'

'Well, he was upset, of course, not knowing you were even in hospital. And it was a very bad line. But they're flying him home immediately, so that's one bit of luck for you.'

I wondered if perhaps luck meant different things to different people.

'What did he say when you told him?'

'Oh, I didn't tell him on the telephone, Mrs Barlow. We never do that. You can't pour a cup of tea down the telephone. He's getting here as soon as he can and I'll talk to him before he sees you.'

'I see.' I felt sick. 'Talking of tea . . .'

'Of course. I expect your mouth feels a bit dry.'

Sister rang the bell before washing my face and hands and tidying the bed. The nurse who answered the summons looked surprised to see her superior indulging in basic nursing. They were well staffed.

'Some tea for Mrs Barlow please, Nurse.'

'Do you take sugar?' she asked me, but before I could answer Sister interrupted with,

'Never ask that question. Bring everything in on the

tray and ask when you are pouring it out. That way you don't forget anything and the patient knows (a) that she's getting what she wants and (b) that it's fresh. I don't know what they teach you girls these days.'

'Oh, it's all right, Sister. I don't need a tray, I'll only spill it. And I don't take sugar thanks, Nurse.'

'Mrs Barlow, tea is served on trays here. I always think of National Health hospitals as living rooms. We private hospitals are the drawing rooms of the health service.'

The nurse went out. Sister fiddled with the drip, wasting time. Then, 'Mrs Barlow, where did you have your biopsy done?'

'At his consulting rooms. Near all the high-class hookers in Shepherd Market. Why?'

'Oh, nothing. They're usually done here, that's all.'

My discretion in exchange for his medical ethics made me answer, 'Everything happened in such a rush and I said I wouldn't come in at all, couldn't spare the time if it turned out to be nothing. So he said O.K., he'd do it there and then, with a local anaesthetic. He's almost got a mini operating theatre there, it's amazing.'

'Did it hurt?'

'No, not at all. Then he sent me home and told me to wait for his phone call. It came the next day and here I am.'

'Here we are,' said the nurse, elbowing the door open.

'That drip can come down in about an hour,' Sister said as she left the room.

'Once that's gone I expect you'll be allowed up. There's none of that in-bed-for-ten-days lark now.'

'Just as well. Who on earth could afford it?'

'Earth's a big place these days. The only reason it keeps going round is because they oil it.'

'Can't wait for an embargo so I can catch up with myself.'

'I'm more optimistic than you. I'm hoping to catch up with somebody else. Tea all right?'

'Considering it's on a tray, it's not at all bad. Do you like working here?'

'No, not really. When I was a student nurse I was always so broke and so tired that I said as soon as I'd qualified and got my hospital badge I'd leave. I didn't actually say that I was going to do private nursing because we looked down on the girls that worked for places like this, agency nurses. I suppose because they got so much more money for, very often, less work. We thought they were gold diggers. But when the time came to leave, when I qualified, I realised that nursing was the only thing I was any good at and yet I was sick to death of being broke. So I slunk into this, hoping that no one would notice. And all I do is keep bumping into people I trained with. They're all at it. So much for integrity. It's overrated.'

'Integrity's O.K. It's when they confuse it with snobbery or piety or use it as an antithesis for greed that it becomes offensive. Real integrity is extremely rare. Anyone can be bought.'

'Right. I was. Money. All that off-duty, choosing when I wanted to work. 'Course I was bought. But I've learned. The thing that will really make me get out is discovering in myself something that I hate. I like people, most people I get time to make contact with. I've marched for freedom in other countries; I believe we're all as good as each other, all that. But suddenly I find myself loathing very rich people, resenting their queue-jumping complacence, nauseated by their Blue Grass and their phony politeness.'

'Of course,' I said politely.

'So I'm going back to my old hospital to staff. Back to real people in a grotty old building that smells of blood and sweat and fear and where we're not automatically issued with compasses so we can work out which way is East. A place where we're all equal and can see each other and where I don't have to use sign language. That's why it's so nice talking to you. We talk the same language and you seem ordinary, if you know what I mean. You're here because you're ill, not because you think your husband might take more notice of you if you're in hospital. Has the injection worked? You look a bit flushed.'

'I must say I do feel a bit woozy.'

'Sorry. I'm so stupid, I never stop babbling. Still, one of my ward sisters once said that that was why my patients got better quickly – to get away from the sound of my voice. See you later.'

'Thanks. And please don't stop talking to me just because I'm falling asleep this time.'

She grinned. 'Watch it or I'll make you a sitting tenant. See you later.'

As she closed the door behind her I didn't know whether to focus on the pain that was receding or the Tim one that was coming closer all the time.

Pethidine took the decision out of my hands and I fell into a restless and unwilling no-man's-land where thought did not exist, although the physical pain followed me there. I was dimly aware of a nurse, a different nurse, taking down my drip but since there was no discomfort there seemed no point in waking up.

I dozed again and finally fell into a deep, deep sleep.

Nineteen

And then it was the next morning and my chatterbox nurse was back again, smiling, but the pain was still there.

Dry mouthed I said, 'That pethidine's not all it's cracked up to be.'

'Hospitals are pleased if you move your bowels. You can't expect them to move with the times as well, be fair.'

'Of course. Any chance of a cup of tea?'

'Sure. I've got an injection for you first. Then tea and a little wash and brush up and another little snooze. How does that sound?'

'Really good.'

The needle went in and out and then there was the sting and I knew that soon the edge would be taken off the pain.

The tea was good, irrigating my mouth so that my lips didn't keep sticking together.

As soon as I had finished the tea the nurse reappeared with a bowl and my washing things. 'Freshen-up time. Make you look pretty.'

'It's that attitude that made us lose so many wars; all that false optimism.'

'Rubbish.'

"'Course it's not rubbish. How are you coping with the queue?'

'Queue? What on earth are you talking about? Soap on your face?'

'No thanks. Makes me go all blotchy.'

'Me too. But some people swear by it.'

'The day I need a bar of soap to make me swear I think I'll give up.'

We both laughed. Then she said, 'Queue. You were talking about a queue.'

'Oh, it's nothing really. I just thought there'd be a great queue of bisexuals out there waiting for me.'

She dried my face. 'Look, Sadie -- can I call you Sadie? -- I don't know what it's like, I can't even imagine it. It must be murder, the nightmare not evaporating with daylight like they're supposed to. And I don't know anyone who can help you cope with it, really come to terms with it. There are people who are supposed to help but I think some of them got their jobs because they failed Humanities. They send black girls, women, out with bright pink tits. Right? So the only person who can help you is going to be you. Not now, not yet, not for a long time. You'll lose friends, lovers, maybe even family. You're like an ethnic minority now. You're a statistic and most people don't like sums. What matters is that you don't let people like that bother you. You've already been crucified, so what can they do? Bang the nails in harder? Sandpaper the cross so you don't get splinters? Some people will cry in front of you. Take no notice. They're selfish voyeurs. People you haven't seen for years will come and see you because they want to know what someone with cancer looks like. The same kind who go to funerals and make out they were really intimate friends. They make me sick. Ignore them. In the end the only person who matters is you. You'll change. You'll never stop living with fear but you will become very strong and independent. You won't need anybody in the end. And don't give me that funny look. It's true.'

I had been looking at the swirly orange curtains, listening carefully and intently.

She continued. 'I mean what I say. I've seen too many people, husbands, lovers. 'Course they're upset. I'm not saying they don't care. But they also get to like their own role. You know, in the pub or the office . . . "Have you heard about poor old John? Shocking isn't it? And so young. Tough old world — saw her only the other week. Bought her a drink as a matter of fact. It's worse for him, of course. All that cooking. None of the other. Ah, here he comes. O.K., old boy? Large Scotch?" They never drink singles again after that. Funnily enough, I'm not a man-hater. I like most men, it's just that I'm not fooled by them any longer. I know, and you know, that women are much much stronger. We don't even have to articulate it; certainties don't have to be discussed. I promise you'll be all right. Not yet. There's a long way to go, a lot of pain and fear and sexual insecurity. There's also the possibility that the man in your life will leave you. A lot of them do. I know nothing about you and your husband . . . but be prepared. And in the end you will become so strong that you will wonder where it came from, that strength. You will be totally independent too. I promise you, when the scar has faded, you won't need anybody on this earth. Have a sleep. I'll see you later.'

I looked towards her and smiled sleepily as I lied, 'Thank you for all that advice. But I have never, ever needed anyone.'

And then I drifted back into my lost world between sleeping and waking, a world where no one could follow me, and isolation formed the boundary.

I was woken up by a tray of food being placed in front

of me, but hunger was another lost sensation and I merely pushed the food around on the plate, disarranged it so that it looked as though I had eaten something.

Then my nurse came in with a broad grin. 'Surprise, surprise. You're having a visitor soon. Your husband rang from Heathrow. He's on his way. Should be here soon. Sister is waiting for him. She'll see him first and then he'll be all yours.'

I tried not to show the panic I was feeling but I obviously failed for she came and sat on my bed.

'Listen. I think you're being fantastic, but you don't have to be. It might be better to save that for when you get home, when you have no choice. In a way hospital is the worst place to come to terms with things — it's all so unreal and you're totally protected and cocooned. And you all try so hard to be brave. Sometimes I wish it could be reversed — you have the operation at home and then come to us when you've got over it and you see the scar and it begins to be real. Because that's when you need people looking after you, helping you, understanding, caring. Not now when the physical pain makes it seem as though that's all that has happened to bring you in here. I'm sorry about the way I went on earlier. I wanted to try and stop you being so brave and funny. Perhaps I even wanted to make you cry, now, while I was here to comfort you. I think you're amazing, the way you tried to make me laugh. Succeeded too. But I can't work out if that's your way of coping with it or if you are trying to protect me. Perhaps it doesn't matter and anyway it's none of my business. But I also know that your husband doesn't know yet, and you're the kind of lady who will care more about protecting him than yourself. What I'm really saying is: great, you protect him — he needs it too — but let me protect you when he's gone. You're my patient, you're the one I care about. O.K., lady? Sorry about all the lectures. I don't give them to everyone, you'll be glad to hear.'

She had been tidying me up all the time she was speaking and as she brushed my hair there was a knock at the door. I looked towards it, knowing that my terror showed in my face, that my eyes had become the kind of fluorescent green Tim had told me they were after Chris's funeral.

The nurse went to the door and opened it a fraction. 'Sorry. Can you wait a couple of minutes? I'll be as quick as possible, promise.'

'Thank you,' I said. 'It must have been very hard to talk to me like that. And thank you for giving me this brief breathing space. I am afraid of seeing him. Can we talk again later? What's your name?'

'Chris.'

My head was so quiet I wouldn't have heard them break the sound barrier.

'Chris? That's amazing. The only woman I've ever been close to in my life was called Chris. I know it's not a particularly uncommon name, but I only ever knew one other. She used to lecture me too. And I took it from her as well. Then she died. Sometimes I feel as though it was my fault, that she mattered too much and in the end I drained everything out of her.' I paused. 'Wish me luck.'

The new Chris went towards the door, and when she spoke it was the wood she studied and not me.

'One last question, and tell me to piss off if you like, but, well, are you O.K., you two? I don't mean divorced or separated, but it's clear you're not looking forward to seeing him.'

'Show him in. And I look forward to our talk later. Really.'

Chris opened the door with a blind wave and a nod of her head. She went out and Tim came in.

He was wearing a double-breasted jacket and my smile vanished as though I were an autistic child who had used those particular muscles by mistake.

'Hello, Tim. Good journey?'

He stood for a moment looking at me, my pale face, the empty drip stand, the drainage bottles hanging from the side of the bed containing blood that looked too red to be real, a redness that I had thought when I first saw them made sense of the Crimson Lake of childhood paint boxes; it would have been exactly the right colour. He tried to look straight up at my face again, my eyes, as though that was the only part of me that mattered, but it was not possible for him to resist looking at my breasts first. He blinked self-consciously several times, hoping that would cover up for him, would blind me to his guilty curiosity, but when finally his eyes came into focus with my own, my gaze was so unwavering that I knew that he knew that I had registered his visual diversion.

As he walked towards me I offered him absolution by saying, 'I know, it doesn't seem real, does it? Not when it hardly shows.' But he had wanted to feel guilty and he frowned as he leant over to kiss me and his 'Sadie, I love you' lacked conviction at the time he probably meant it the most.

He sat on the edge of the bed nervously, dragging on the drainage tubes so that I cried out in pain and pushed him away.

'Sorry. Sorry, Tim. Come round the other side. There's a chair there. Sorry. I didn't mean to yell at you.'

As he sat in the chair, I smiled at him. 'You're very quiet. And very brown. How was it out there?'

'O.K. Hard work, but O.K.'

'I didn't think you'd even have got the message yet.'

'They have telex machines. And they're very efficient when something matters. I've always said they're a good firm to work for.' I probably imagined the slight accusation in his voice.

There was another silence. Tim got up and went to the window, looking out as though he could see something interesting the other side of the opaque glass. I leaned back against the pillows, wondering why his silhouette was so familiar, and why that familiarity hurt more than my physical mutilation. I called his name and as he turned towards me the tears he had been trying to hide came spilling out, unstoppable and angry.

I held my arm out to him and he moved towards me as though it was his life that had so savagely and un-expectedly altered course. He wept against my face while I stroked his hair, my fingers barely registering the texture that had so delighted me once. His crying became rougher, noisier, less private, until it obliterated all sensibilities and his head dragged down gradually, harshly against my cheek, my chin, my neck, towards its accustomed resting place on my breast. I lifted his lost heavy head across on to my right breast where the comfort cushioned his despair and he gradually began to come to the end of the weeping that I was not able to begin. I held his head tightly against me, anxious to delay his moment of realisation for as long as possible, knowing that sometimes the physical manifestation of distress was sufficient to render the initial cause tem-porarily unimportant. Besides, I didn't want him to recover yet. It was far easier to give comfort than to be comforted with the reasons why comfort was necessary in the first place.

Soon the injection would wear off and the physical pain would dominate again, and then everything would be easier, less clearly defined. And Tim wouldn't have to bear it.

Gradually his silence and even breathing became louder

144

than his tears ever had been. He remained where he was until his eyes were less swollen, and at first when he tried to lift his head I held it down, stroking his hair as though comforting a child. I was afraid, at last, of too many things. Afraid of the future, afraid of what I had done, afraid of meeting his eyes in case he began to understand. We stayed like that, in that Madonna and Child pose, until the physical pain was really strong again, dominating all other feeling. Then I relaxed my hands and his head left the safety of my warmth and softness for the danger of independence. He straightened up and looked at me as though awakening from a refreshing snooze.

'Ouch. Stiff neck.'

'Here, let me massage it for you.' I weakly rubbed my one usable hand up and down his neck and shoulders.

'Thank you. Oh, that's lovely. Mmmmmmmm.'

After a moment I stopped. 'Sorry. That's your lot.'

'That's fine now. How are you?'

'All right. Apart from the pain.'

'Where does it hurt?'

'Where they operated. And my arms.'

'Your arms? Why's that?'

'Dunno. The drip was this side but the other one hurts more.'

'It's bound to, I suppose.'

'Why?'

'Well, it's near. Nerves are probably involved. Come to think of it, Sister told me your arm would hurt quite a lot.'

'What else did she say?'

'That you'd had an operation. You know, the one you've had . . . '

'Did she tell you exactly what they've done?'

'Yes.'

'What have they done?'

145

'Don't you know?'

'I want to hear it again. In case it's a mistake, what they told me. I was quite drowsy. And you know what an optimist I am. And how bad my memory is. You once told me it was your role in life to cheer me up, to make me happy.'

'Sadie, please don't.'

'What have they done to me, Tim?'

'You've had a mastectomy.'

'What exactly is that?'

'Why are you being so cruel?'

'What exactly is a mastectomy Tim?'

'They have removed your breast.'

'All of it?'

'All of it.'

'Which one?'

'The left one.'

'Your favourite.'

I looked at his misery to see if there was something about such an expression that could be misinterpreted or ignored as he had mine, as though nothing diagnostic showed on an unhappy face.

'I only said it'd be my favourite if I were forced to choose. And I only said it once.'

'Well, that's one problem you won't have now.'

'No. And we can still do it. I asked her that, so don't worry.'

'You asked her that? Today, when you were told for the first time?'

'Of course I did. It's important.'

'But she's Irish.'

Tim stood up. 'I must go now. She said ten minutes and it's been nearly an hour already. You look tired.'

'I am.'

'I don't know. I can't turn my back on you for a

minute. It won't make any difference, you know. I love you for your head as well as your body. And I've always thought an extra hand would be useful.'

'We could get some badges printed.'

'Saying what?'

'One is fun.'

'Stop it, Sadie. I love you. I'll see you again this evening. We'll manage. We've got each other and I fell in love with you, not your breasts.'

'Why? What was wrong with them?'

'Nothing. Don't be silly.'

He didn't seem to know what to say next, and then he looked at my empty locker.

'Anything you want brought in tonight?'

'A nightie, if you can get one that opens down the front.'

'Right. How about some fruit?'

'Tomorrow perhaps.'

'All right. Nothing else?'

'Oh, I'd love some Perrier water.'

'Sure. I must go. Oh, by the way, where's the car and have you got the keys?'

'No.'

'Oh, are they at home? I'll find them.'

'You won't.'

'Don't say you've lost them again?'

'No, no. I've sold it.'

'You've what?'

'I've sold the car.'

'For God's sake, have you gone mad? Why on earth did you do that?'

'I needed the money.'

Twenty

The remaining days in hospital passed quite comfortably
once the drainage tubes were out. I had screamed when
the first one was removed and Sister had put her head
round the door of the treatment room, frowning first at
me and then at Chris. 'I'm sorry,' I said. 'It felt as though
it was sewn in. It really did hurt. But I'm sorry about all
that noise.'

Sister nodded in an all-right-but-don't-let-it-happen-
again way and then closed the door with a slight bang.
Chris made a face after her. 'She ought to work in a
taxidermist's, not a hospital. I'm sorry I hurt you. Nearly
finished now. The other one will probably come out
tomorrow or the next day and that won't be so bad
because it's shorter. It's healing beautifully, look.'

'I'll take your word for it,' I replied, staring at the
ceiling, terrified of looking at the scar in case it was
really there. Chris was silent, concentrating on covering
up the unseeable.

As she helped me back into bed she said, 'Has Dr
Zhivago, as you call him, told you when you can go
home?'

'No. He said something about going after ten days and
then coming back to have the stitches out, but it was all a
bit vague. He's supposed to be coming to see me, so I
hope he'll be a bit more definite then. Oh, that's nice. It's
really nice to get into bed sometimes.'

'He won't be coming to see you here, Sadie. You know he's retired now, and he's gone on holiday. He won't be back for over a week.' I must have looked shocked and alarmed for Chris added, 'Don't worry. He'll have left instructions with Sister. You won't have to wait for him to come back, if that's what you're thinking. I'll find out when we have the report and let you know. Is Tim coming to see you today?'

'As far as I know. He didn't say he wasn't.'

'How is he? Everything all right?'

I felt my face close up. 'Fine. Thank you.'

There was a brief pause while Chris waited to see if I wanted to say anything else, but I stared out of the window as if I was alone.

'I'll leave you then. Try and have a nap. See you later.'

I knew that I was making Chris unhappy and even that she was a little afraid of my coldness, and there were times when I wanted to call out after her and beg her to come back and help me stop being so afraid. But I didn't because this Chris was so very like the other one that I would have ended up telling her the truth and neither of us could have handled that.

Tim came every day to see me. He looked as though he had fallen to pieces and been put back together in rather a hurry. After both the drainage tubes were out, I spent most of the time wishing that I was in a ward with other people. I felt as lonely as my remaining breast, and even reading was no consolation. I never talked to Chris again in the familiar way that had given us both so much pleasure before Tim had returned from the Gulf. Now, if Chris said or asked something too intrusive – and she didn't give up easily – I simply froze her out before the offending sentence or question was completed, and I believe she began to find excuses not to come into my room.

Tim, loving me, always brought flowers or gifts with him, and even managed a few jokes towards the end of my stay there. Dr Zhivago had indeed gone on holiday and I was glad that he had not charged me, that I was in no way contributing to his sun tan. He had told Sister that I could go home after ten days, come back and have the stitches out and see him again the following week when he was going to be back in town winding up his private practice.

On the morning of the day I was going home Chris came into my room, ostensibly to say goodbye. I hadn't seen her for a couple of days and we exchanged trivial pleasantries for a moment or two and then she said, 'Sadie, I'm sorry for whatever I've done or said to upset you. I wish you'd tell me what it was so that I could explain or at least understand so that I don't say it again. This not knowing is driving me crazy.'

I was silent and still, frozen into the realisation that I could not blame Eva or Chris or Tim or Dr Zhivago, that I alone had generated this emotional holocaust and that it would contaminate everyone I came into contact with for the rest of my life. Chris was the first of the casualties and the bewilderment on her innocent face devastated me. I wanted to reach out and touch her hand and turn her into the other Chris so that none of this would have happened.

The silence was elastic, as though there were no breaking point.

'Well, I'll leave you to it. I've learned my lesson. I'll never talk to another patient the way I talked to you. I'm so sorry. I really got it wrong. I thought I recognised something in you and you would want me to acknowledge that recognition. You seemed special, I liked you and I wanted to help. I'm sorry that I didn't.' She looked defeated and gave a funny kind of shrug as she added, 'Well, Sister will be pleased. About me not talking to patients, I mean. Goodbye, Sadie. I'll think about you often. I hope everything will go well. Please remember that I said I was sorry. For whatever I've done. I should never have talked to you the way I did, I realise that now. At the time I thought not being honest would demean you . . . you seemed above trivia. In a funny kind of way, thank you. For teaching me to shut up. Take care.'

When she had her hand on the door handle she suddenly turned back towards me and the diamond points of unshed tears in my eyes must have been what made it possible for her to add, 'But it's not just the mastectomy is it?'

I closed my eyes briefly and opened my mouth to say, No it's not just the mastectomy, it's all sorts of unsayable things and I recognise you too, with love, the way women can sometimes and I've done the most terrible thing and please may we talk? But I never said anything because the door opened and Tim walked in and stood between Chris and me like a flood barrier, smiling with delight because I was coming home. My hand, which had been half held out to Chris, fell back on the bed and the laser beam that had seemed to shine between our eyes disappeared.

Chris closed the door quietly behind her.

Tim's exuberance was less immediately infectious than perhaps he would have liked. He had gone to so much trouble though, planning this day with such thrilled anticipation, that eventually, loving him, I pushed the misery of the second Chris to the back of my mind, put it on ice until I could be alone with it, and concentrated on Tim.

As we were about to leave the room a secretary appeared with a bill in a sealed envelope. I took my cheque book out, turning towards the locker and away from Tim, trying to open the envelope without him seeing. The secretary bird said, 'I shouldn't open that until you get home. We don't want you having a relapse, do we? You've got a week's grace. Time to sell your car. Or flee the country.'

'Don't give me ideas; I might do both,' I gabbled, desperately trying to get away from the subject. My human overdraft facility laughed inordinately loudly and it seemed as though she might stand there between us, for ever giggling, if Tim hadn't spoken.

'Talking of cars,' he said, guiding me towards the door so that all three of us had to leave if we were to avoid a collision, 'I told the meter maid I'd only be five minutes. She had a stop watch with a double yellow line round it so I'm taking her seriously.' This forced the secretary into further convulsions, which necessitated her standing still to maintain a vertical position and we were able to escape towards Sister's office. Chris was in there as well and I hesistated a moment until Sister, astonishingly, said, 'Good God, you'd think hyenas were an endangered species, the way that secretary carries on,' and laughter punctuated the tension for as long as it took to hand over the chocolates and hand cream Tim had bought. I noticed that it was Blue Grass. I was given an appointment to return in five days to have the stitches out and while Sister was writing out the card another patient rang her bell imperiously and Chris left to answer it, so it was quite easy then to say goodbye to Sister alone and step into the waiting lift.

As we came out on the ground floor, the porter who had welcomed me in three languages bade me farewell in English.

Outside was a gleaming, shining, brilliant new Rolls-Royce with a matching chauffeur, and a traffic warden at either end protecting it from less elitist forms of transport. I hovered, forgetting and looking for the Mini,

152

and was amazed when the chauffeur of the Silver Shadow Mark II got out and opened the door, gesturing to us to enter. In the back were flowers and chocolates and champagne and magazines and I found myself sitting down with a glass in my hand before I quite knew what was happening. I looked briefly through the back window, that I had expected to be made of smoked glass, at the telephone box from which I had sent the telegram. It appeared to be extremely small, as if I had drunk Alice's medicine before looking, and then I realised that we were moving away from it. The car was so smooth and silent that the shifting perspectives were the only indications of the speed at which we were travelling. Feeling slightly sick, I looked at Tim but his huge smile of delight was so infectious that it had to be rewarded. I reached out for his hand, pressed his cool, smooth fingers and was astonished to feel desire flooding through me so strongly that I felt I must be changing colour. Tim pressed my fingers back very sharply and I knew that he felt it too.

'This is the life, eh?' he said after a further electrical impulse apparently opened the window without either of us touching it.

'What's happening? Where are we going?'

'Shopping. Then home. O.K.?'

We stopped as suddenly as we had started, the only evidence being the people on the pavement who seemed suddenly to be running. As further confirmation, the chauffeur opened the door and gestured us towards an incredibly expensive underwear shop. Inside, Tim explained to the girl what it was we wanted.

'We don't really cater for that,' she said, 'but if you like you can see if any of our normal ones fit.'

Tim began a slow burn of anger and I wanted to leave.

We looked through rows of matching bras and knickers. Tim picked out two sets, one grey and one probably called blush pink, both trimmed with coffee-coloured lace. 'What size do you think you are?' Tim whispered to me. Having hardly ever worn a bra since I left school, I shrugged. 'No idea.'

He held the pink one up against me and the salesgirl gasped and ushered us into a cubicle so that we had to try it on. This made me irritable as it was still uncomfortable getting dressed and undressed, so that when the first one was too tight and the second too loose it was only the gentleness of Tim's hands that made me persevere. As we came back into the shop to pick out the middle size I felt the girl look at my breast as though it was in an exhibition. In retaliation I looked at the garments as if they were export rejects, one of those small, spiteful gestures that is eminently satisfying but totally wasted.

I sat on a chair, expecting to be asked to stand up.

Tim went over to the cash desk, and Miss Two-tits-and-proud-of-it wrote out the bill and then read the total out loud. I looked around the shop, convinced that two tiny bras and small knickers could not possibly be £57.30, but Tim had written out the cheque and collected the small package before I had time to protest. As we walked out of the shop guilt made me say, 'Well, they are real silk. Or satin.'

Back in our luxury limousine, driving away from Bond Street, Tim opened the bag so that I could have another look. Curiously I looked at the label to see what size I was, but I never did find out because I was blinded by another, hidden, label that said '100% Polyester'. 'Ever felt you've been ripped off?' I muttered to Tim, hoping that would ignite his anger, but he just smiled; he would have spent twice that if it would make me feel more confident.

I lay back against the cushions and fell asleep. We must have stopped at a couple more shops because when we got home there were several more packages. I stumbled going up the steps and headed straight for the bedroom, exhaustion guiding my footsteps. I lay on the bed and fell instantly asleep.

Much, much later I woke up and fumbled my way to first the loo and then the bathroom. Stuck up on the mirror was the address of Tim's head office in London and the telegram I had sent him. 'THERE IS A LUMP ON ONE OF YOUR BABIES THEY OPERATE TOMORROW ST CLAIR'S HOSPITAL LOVE SADIE.'

When I got back into bed Tim was there, reaching out for me. It was too soon, I felt like a bloke, I was afraid. And then he made it possible by saying, 'Come here. I feel afraid too. So let's get it over with.'

Twenty-one

While I had slept in the car on the way home Tim had shopped for clothes for me. Tight jeans, loose shirts, waistcoats, gathered tops and dresses. Pretty, easy clothes that made me feel neither like a butch bisexual nor a mutilated woman.

We made love a few times in the days before I had to go back and have my stitches out, although we couldn't press our bodies hard together because of the dressing. The absent nipple caused considerable phantom pains, as though it were being erased with sandpaper, but the other side of that coin was the equally considerable phantom pleasure generated if Tim found the right imaginary area. So an anticipated loss became an un-expected gain.

He had hired the Rolls again for the return visit to the hospital. He hadn't mentioned the sale of the Mini, except obliquely by saying that his lady must travel in style from now on, and by his lofty attitude to any car that cost less than eight thousand pounds it was clear that he had ordered something rather special. I could have provoked him under pressure, but I didn't want to know yet. It didn't seem to matter. I couldn't decide what to wear because I kept wondering if Chris would be there to take my stitches out, and in the end Tim had to come in and hand me some jeans and a shirt.

I felt less afraid walking into the hospital this time.

They had done their worst and Tim's arm around me would ward off all evils. Actually it was a good feeling going back, knowing that it would be for such a short time. Sister looked more Irish today and less pleased to see me than the hand cream should warrant.

She ushered me into the treatment room, pointing Tim towards a chair outside and virtually slamming the door in his face.

Inside I undressed and lay on the hard couch. While Sister was washing her hands I asked her if Chris was on duty.

'I take it you mean Staff Nurse Taylor? She's not here this morning. She's got her divorce today.'

'Divorce? I didn't know she was married.'

'I'm not sure that she did. And anyway she wasn't for long. Now just relax. That's it. Oh, before I forget, Nurse Taylor asked me to give you this,' and she pulled a creased envelope out of her pocket and put it in my hand. I stuffed it in the pocket of my jeans while she scrubbed her hands again.

'Right. Big breaths. Good. Now this might be cold but it won't hurt. More of a pulling, you'll feel. Here we go.'

I stared hard at the familiar ceiling, seeing the top of the frilly starched cap out of the corner of my eye, like a bleached bat.

It did hurt, quite badly, but remembering the earlier contempt, I stayed silent. As long as I didn't have to see it it hadn't happened. I closed my eyes wondering, since Tim gave me pleasure and this only pain, what sensation a suckling baby would have created. And then a last gasp and it was all over. Nothing to it.

I sat up with some assistance and swung my legs round. I climbed down the two small steps and reached for my blouse, noticing the reflection of my arm in the mirror. Habit made me move towards it and there was a brief moment when I imagined that Sister was trying to stop me and then my own reflection obliterated the royal blue arm.

There appeared to be some mistake. I looked behind me and then in front, looking for my place in the queue. I frowned in bewilderment at Sister. Where was her arm now, when I needed it? Then I met her gaze and began to understand the brusqueness, which was entirely missing from her eyes now. They seemed to be attempting to bore strength into me and indeed might have succeeded if the mirror had not been so magnetic. I pulled the shirt over my head but it was so fine and the clinical light so bright that I could see through it. Too late to pretend now. It began to be real.

The livid purple scar was the only indication that I had once had two breasts and I let the shirt fall and pressed both hands very hard against the scar, trying to cover it up and maintain the pretence. My face on top looked like Munch's 'The Scream' and soon I began to sound like it as well. Tim opened the door and it was Sister's face he must have seen first, not trying to hide her compassion now, guiding him towards me. He put his arms round me, holding me as close as possible and saying, 'It's all right, it doesn't matter, we're still us, that's what's important.'

I pushed him fiercely away. 'It does matter, we're not still us, you don't know, you haven't seen it, it cannot be dismissed. Is this what you married? Look.' And I pulled my shirt up, standing back so that he could really see. He reached out to touch it lightly and I stared at him, waiting to see if he recoiled, if his hand faltered before making the connection. He ran his fingers down its livid shiny length as though touching something fragile and precious. 'That's incredible. I thought it was going to look like a road works. It's almost beautiful.' There was no doubting his sincerity; I could not fault him, despite my stinging face and open mouthed sobs.

Sister returned with her equivalent of sympathy, tea. On a tray. She gave Tim two appointment cards for Dr Zhivago, one for me for next week and one for him for the following day, but I didn't see him put them in his pocket, knew nothing about them until it was too late. When the tea was poured Sister said, 'The lady from Surgical Appliances is here. I asked her to come up to save you getting lost in the basement. I'll show her in now. Don't worry, she's seen all this before.'

As deaf and dumb as an unborn child, I hardly noticed at first that Tim's arms were no longer supporting me and I slumped towards the mirror, resting my flooded face gratefully against its coolness.

The lady from Surgical Appliances opened her brief-case on the treatment couch and it was that sight that finally turned my tears into hiccoughs of desolate despair. The case was full of breasts of all shapes and sizes with an inert and disembodied life of their own, like a prize-winning hamper in a *Playboy* competition or a necro-philiac snack bar. The travelling saleswoman looked at me through half-closed eyes. 'Let's see. You look like a size two to me. The question is, are you heart-shaped or pear-shaped?' and I was jolted into a sudden and dangerously noisy silence. If she says I'm pear-shaped, that's it, I give up, I thought to myself, but I actually mumbled it so that Tim could decipher the words and I almost heard him hold his breath and say a silent Please God, Please God, Please God. Then we heard the earthly pronouncement. 'Hearts are trumps.'

I could not resist a small, triumphant glance at Tim, who smiled his proud acknowledgment before putting his arms round me again.

'The trouble is, I haven't got any heart-shaped size twos,' said the lady, giving with one hand taking back with the other. 'I'll have to order one for you. Let me have your phone number and I'll ring you when it arrives. Actually I'll order half a dozen; I've had two in the last week.'

'How long will it take?' said Tim, practically.

'Oh, a couple of weeks. Maybe three. It all depends on the post from Banbury.'

I broke the ensuing silence. 'Are they sent first or second class?'

'Do you know, I've never looked. Mind you, with all these cuts I expect it's second by now, if it hasn't always been.'

Tim spoke next. 'Well, can I go and pick it up? It's not far, Banbury.'

'Oh no, you mustn't do that. There'd be a strike, I should think, and besides you might set a precedent and then where would we be?'

And so one of the most traumatic psychological moments of my life was snatched away from me before I could wallow in it, and turned into a black bureaucratic farce where the good fairies were on a go slow.

I gave a mirthless laugh that must have been more disturbing than all the earlier hysteria. 'This gives booby trap letter bombs a whole new dimension. Please take me home, Tim. Pity the Post Office don't send all their bills out from Banbury. That would cut their profits. Two to three weeks. Unbelievable.'

Tim followed me out, aiming a slightly apologetic glance at the now closed suitcase. I chatted brightly and dangerously all the way home, not giving Tim a chance to say anything. But once the front door was closed behind us it was another story. I reverted to the devastating hysteria that the hospital had been unable to contain. I couldn't stay away from the mirror and soon the shirt was discarded altogether so that even the scar and the remaining breast were covered in tears and mucous. Tim let me cry, hovering awkwardly, knowing that it would never be this bad again, hoping I would not ever be ashamed of for once in my life showing what I felt. In the end, as they had to, the tears gave way to a restless uneasy sleep where Tim eventually joined me, impatient for the equality that oblivion guaranteed.

The next morning Tim got up early, leaving me asleep. He left me a note saying that he had to go to a meeting at head office about going out to the Gulf more permanently and for me to think about it; perhaps a change of scenery would do me good? And he loved me. I awoke about midday, enjoying the few seconds that belonged to that moment, before yesterday insistently intruded, setting the pattern for the rest of my life. I didn't see Tim's note immediately and loneliness made me panic about the future. I had some tea, wishing my arm hurt less, and it was when I took my cup into the sitting room that I saw his note. Before, I had always preferred to stay at home, for there had been the fertility clinic and there had been Chris, but now travelling with him seemed a wonderful idea and I drank my tea quickly and then went and started looking through my summer clothes, discarding those that the mastectomy rendered unsuitable, bundling them into a big black bag before they had time to remind me of earlier, happier days.

The afternoon post brought a letter from the priest of the church where Eva was buried, acknowledging the one I had sent only recently telling him that Chris was dead. He sent his commiserations and an invitation for me to visit the now completed headstone guarding and identifying my mother's grave. I felt curiously content and did not realise for some time how late it was growing.

When I flicked the television on and the nine o'clock news came to life I had a frightening premonition of disaster. Something must be very wrong for Tim to be this late. The news was followed by a programme about breast cancer, the kind where irresponsible journalism masquerades as the horse's mouth. I switched off. I was lying in the bath when I heard the front door slam behind Tim and I called out to him in relieved delight, 'I'm in here Tim, in the bathroom. It's faded a bit already, I swear. Come and see. Tim?'

He didn't come in immediately. I heard him going into the kitchen and clumsily banging around. There was a splashing noise and muffled swearing and then the clink of ice cubes, and a drink seemed a wonderful idea. I scooped up a handful of bubbles and transferred them from my knees to my chest before, less exposed, calling out to him again. 'Tim? Bathroom. Tell me all. Are we going to live in the sun?'

Still he didn't come. He banged his way into the sitting room again and I heard him flick the television from one channel to another and then off and then the record player thumped out with early Dylan, the first album we had listened to together, the one with 'Just Like a Woman' on it. My sense of foreboding grew worse.

I got out of the bath as best as I could with one hand, hoping now that he wouldn't come in until I was covered up by a nightdress. I had hardly worn one since I had been with Tim and it was oddly comforting, a reminder of innocence and timetables, this grown-up world a lifetime away.

I went into the bedroom and brushed my hair and sprayed myself with Madame Rochas. I felt slightly sick.

I went into the kitchen and poured myself a whisky with lots of ice to make it look as though I was having a bigger drink than I really was.

'Just Like a Woman' was playing now, and then there was a sudden thump and the sound of the needle being dragged across the album, a noise to set the teeth on edge.

I stood in the doorway. Tim was hardly recognisable. His face was blotchy with alcohol and tears, his hair spiky and damp, everything totally out of focus.

'Hello, Tim,' was all I could think of to say.

'Hello, Sadie. You should change your name. Sadistic would do for starters.' He looked in my direction. I still didn't understand.

'What's happened, Tim? What's the matter?'

'You. You're the matter. Sadist. Sadie.'

'Tim . . .'

'Don't Tim me. Makes it seem we knew each other.'

I sat on the arm of a chair facing him, before my legs gave way.

'How did you get on? Let's go abroad. I went through my summer things. They'll be fine.'

'I'm going. Day after tomorrow. Not you.'

'What?'

'Not you. Dr Zhivago sends his love.'

'Dr Zhivago?'

'Dr Zhivago.' Tim began crying noisily, desperately, as though, like me, he had hardly wept before, not even as a child. I closed my eyes, terror transforming my nausea into something unrecognisable and indescribable, as though brilliant sunshine were shining through the top of my head on to my brain.

'Why, Sadie, why?'

My mouth was so dry that my tongue stuck to my palette.

'Answer me. How could you do that? You're mad. Mad and sick and wicked.'

I swilled a little whisky around in my mouth, trying to

163

substitute it for saliva so that I could say, 'Chris and Eva. The last link in the chain. Going full circle. Make of all those parts a whole. And Margie and your baby.' But the words didn't come out and my silence infuriated Tim, who started shouting now.

'Cancer, Sadie. That's what you're playing games with. Cancer. Something that kills thousands of innocent people. Play games with backache or 'flu or toothache or migraine if you have to play games at all. But — cancer. That is gross. What's the matter with you? Not enough attention? You're mad. No. Not mad. Criminally insane. And Zhivago. Oh, he did you proud. Kept on bluffing. Until I threatened to stop the cheque to the hospital going through. He talked then all right. Told you they'd do anything for money. Why, why, why?'

I retched and the taste of bile flooded my mouth with saliva and I could speak again. 'All the other things that made me a woman were useless. I thought one more lie would make me the same as the rest of you. Like Chris. To feel some of her pain. Balance the books. And Eva. Tried to make sense of their lives. Tried to understand. Full circle.'

'Chris? Eva? Who's Eva? You can fool Zhivago, but not me. You don't know what you're talking about any more. He's an old man. I won't report him. He's retired now and you signed a consent form. He's smashed my life, no point smashing his. What's left of it.' Drunk and fumbly, he managed to stand up. He staggered towards the door, shambling, shattered, defeated.

I followed him into the hall, knowing that it was too late, but unable to admit it. He kept missing the front door handle. 'Shall I tell you something, Sadistic? I'm ashamed I ever knew you.' And now he had the door open. 'I'm going now. Goodbye.'

It wasn't quite too late, I thought. He was half-way out of the door.

'Margie or Flora rang. Pregnant. Can't tell Stork from butter?'

I still had my trump card to play, even though he hadn't seemed to know what I had just said.

'Tim. My Tim . . . '

He looked back, a glimmer of hope, wanting something from me that might make sense of the senseless, justify everything. I began the sentence that would make everything all right. Half-way through it he spat at me, and on the final syllable he slammed the door. I repeated it, for perhaps he had not properly heard.

'Tim. Tim. I did it because I love you.'

Twenty-two

'I did it because I love you,' Eva had said and so had Tim. At the time they had hurt me, and I had forgiven them, thought love a reasonable and honest justification. Why, then, did it not work the other way round? It should have meant to Tim what it had meant to me. He should have listened and believed and forgiven me. There had been a time when he had begged me to say I loved him, but I hadn't, because I wanted it to be the truest thing I ever said.

He hasn't come back. I had a brief formal letter from a lawyer, laying out the generous financial arrangements he had made for me with the proviso that I contact him only through his legal advisors. And I had a note from Tim himself, just saying that for my information I might like to know that the American girl who had rung had been the widow of the friend who had died in Scotland and that she was ringing to say that at least she had something of him. The thanks were for Tim's help in looking after all the funeral arrangements. The postmark was Bahrain.

Some weeks after he left I had found the envelope from Chris the nurse. It contained a slip of paper with her name and address and telephone number. Eva. Chris. Chris. I had burned it; it had seemed too like one of those chain letters that guarantee you good luck if you don't break the chain.

Now I don't feel anything much. Sometimes I used to do a visual trick that reminded me of the days when everything seemed possible: I would stand in front of the mirror looking at my fading scar and then, half closing my eyes, I would look at the breast that was left, the right one, and then very quickly look at the scar and sometimes I could for a second superimpose the image of the other on to it so that I looked normal again.

I tried it this morning but it didn't work, I was unable to look away from the real breast, to transfer its visual image and pretend that it had never happened. I looked for a long time, before I touched, not wanting my fingers to corroborate the visual evidence. On the outer side, near my arm, was a dimpled lump, about an inch in diameter. When I touched it, I felt a desolate sense of triumph.

It had, after all, been only a matter of time.